Candy Fairies

3-Books-in-1! #2

DON'T MISS THE REST OF THE CANDY FAIRIES SERIES!

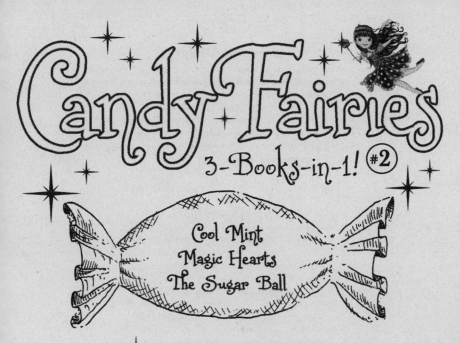

Candy Fairies

3-Books-in-1! #2

Cool Mint
Magic Hearts
The Sugar Ball

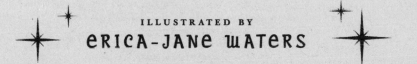

HELEN PERELMAN

ILLUSTRATED BY
ERICA-JANE WATERS

ALADDIN
NEW YORK   LONDON   TORONTO   SYDNEY   NEW DELHI

This book is a work of fiction. Any references to historical events, real people, or real places are used fictitiously. Other names, characters, places, and events are products of the author's imagination, and any resemblance to actual events or places or persons, living or dead, is entirely coincidental.

ALADDIN

An imprint of Simon & Schuster Children's Publishing Division
1230 Avenue of the Americas, New York, New York 10020
This Aladdin paperback edition October 2016
Cool Mint text copyright © 2010 by Helen Perelman
Cool Mint interior illustrations copyright © 2010 by Erica-Jane Waters
Magic Hearts text copyright © 2011 by Helen Perelman
Magic Hearts interior illustrations copyright © 2011 by Erica-Jane Waters
The Sugar Ball text copyright © 2011 by Helen Perelman
The Sugar Ball interior illustrations copyright © 2011 by Erica-Jane Waters
Cover illustration copyright © 2010 by Erica-Jane Waters
All rights reserved, including the right of reproduction in whole or in part in any form.
ALADDIN is a trademark of Simon & Schuster, Inc., and related logo
is a registered trademark of Simon & Schuster, Inc.
For information about special discounts for bulk purchases, please contact
Simon & Schuster Special Sales at 1-866-506-1949 or business@simonandschuster.com.
The Simon & Schuster Speakers Bureau can bring authors to your live event.
For more information or to book an event contact the Simon & Schuster Speakers Bureau
at 1-866-248-3049 or visit our website at www.simonspeakers.com.
Series designed by Karin Paprocki
Interior designed by Michael Rosamilia
The text of this book was set in Berthold Baskerville Book.
Manufactured in the United States of America 0916 OFF
2 4 6 8 10 9 7 5 3 1
Library of Congress Control Number 2016939443
ISBN 978-1-4814-8566-1 (pbk)
ISBN 978-1-4424-0963-7 (*Cool Mint* eBook)
ISBN 978-1-4424-0824-1 (*Magic Hearts* eBook)
ISBN 978-1-4424-0826-5 (*The Sugar Ball* eBook)
These titles were previously published individually by Aladdin.

Contents

Cool Mint

For Nathan, my sweet

CHAPTER
1

Cool Ride

A cool morning breeze blew through Marshmallow Marsh. Dash, the smallest Mint Fairy in Sugar Valley, was very excited. She had been working on her new sled all year, and now her work was done. Finally the sled was ready to ride. And just in time! Sledding season was about to begin.

Many fairies in Sugar Valley didn't like the cool months as much as Dash. Each season in Sugar Valley had its own special flavors and candies— and Dash loved them all. She was a small fairy with a large appetite!

Dash was happiest during the winter. All the mint candies were grown in the chilly air that swept through Sugar Valley during the wintertime. She enjoyed the refreshing mint scents and the clean white powdered sugar. But for her, the thrill of competing was the sweetest part of the season. She had waited all year for this chance to try out her new sled!

The Marshmallow Run was one of the brightest highlights of the winter for Dash. The sled race was one of the most competitive and challenging races in Sugar Valley. And for the past two years, Dash had won first place. But this year was different. This year Dash wanted to be the fastest fairy in the kingdom—and set a new speed record. No fairy had been able to beat Pep the Mint Fairy's record in years. He had stopped racing now and was one of Princess Lolli's closest advisers. But no one had come close to breaking his record.

Dash had carefully picked the finest candy to make her sled the fastest. While many of her fairy friends had been playing in the fields, she had been hard at work. She was sure that the slick red licorice blades with iced tips and the cool peppermint seat was going to make her new sled ride perfectly. If she was going to break the record this year, she'd need all the help she could get.

Dash looked around. No one else was on the slopes at this early hour. She took a deep breath. The conditions were perfect for her test run. "Here I go," she said.

On her new sled Dash glided down the powdered sugar trail that led into the white marshmallow peaks. It was a tricky and sticky course, but Dash had done the run so many times she knew every turn and dip of the lower part of the Frosted Mountains. She steered her sled easily and sped down the mountain. The iced tips on the sled's blades made all the difference! She was picking up great speed as she neared the bottom of the slope.

When she reached the finish line, she checked her watch. Had she done it? Had she beat the Candy Kingdom record?

"Holy peppermint!" she cried.

Dash couldn't believe how close she was to beating her best time. She had to shave off a few more seconds to break the record, but this was the fastest run she had ever had. Dash grinned. *This year is my year,* she thought happily.

Suddenly a sugar fly landed on her shoulder with a note. Dash recognized the neat handwriting of her friend Raina. Raina was a Gummy Fairy and always followed the rules of the Fairy Code Book. She was a gentle and kind fairy who was also a very good friend.

"Raina told you that you'd find me here, huh?" Dash said to the small fly.

The tiny messenger nodded.

Dash opened Raina's note. "She thinks she has to remind me about Sun Dip," Dash said to the fly. She shook her head, smiling.

Sun Dip was a time when all the fairies came together to talk about their day and share their candy. Dash loved the large feast of the day and enjoyed sharing treats with her friends. Now that the weather was turning colder, her mint candies were all coming up from the ground. Peppermint Grove was sprouting peppermint sticks and mint suckers for the winter season.

Dash looked up and saw the sun was still high above the top of the mountains. She had time for a couple more runs. She was so close to beating the record. How could she stop now?

"Tell Raina that I'll be there as soon as I can," Dash told the sugar fly. The tiny fly nodded. Then he flew off toward Gummy Forest to deliver the message.

Flapping her wings, Dash flew back to the top of the slope with her new sled. She had to keep practicing.

My friends will understand, she thought.

As she reached the top of the slope, Dash could think about only one thing. Wouldn't all the fairies be surprised when the smallest Mint Fairy beat the record? Dash couldn't wait to see their faces! And to get the first-place prize! The sweet success of winning the Marshmallow

Run was a large chocolate marshmallow trophy. It was truly a delicious way to mark the sweet victory of winning the race.

With those happy, sweet thoughts in her head, Dash took off. Cool wind on her face felt great as she picked up speed down the mountain. A few more runs and she'd beat the record, sure as sugar.

This year everyone would be talking about Dash—the fastest Mint Fairy ever!

CHAPTER 2

Frosty Sun Dip

Dash flapped her wings quickly, racing toward Red Licorice Lake. She hoped her friends would still be there. She knew that the sun had already dipped below the mountains—and that she was very late. But wait till they heard her great news!

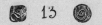

As she neared the sugar beach, Dash saw Raina looking up at the sky. She was pointing toward the Frosted Mountains. "The sun has been down for a long time," she stated. "Soon the stars will be out."

"No sign of Dash?" Melli the Caramel Fairy asked. Squinting, she searched for any sign of her friend.

"Dash has never missed Sun Dip," Cocoa added. The Chocolate Fairy flew up in the sky and scouted the area. "No sign of her."

"Here I am!" Dash called out. Her cheeks were red as she rushed over to her friends. "I know I'm late," she said, starting to explain.

"Let me guess, you were on the slopes?" Berry asked. The Fruit Fairy fluttered her pink wings and settled down on her blanket. "I think all

that time on the other side of Chocolate River is getting to you, Dash. You've never missed a Sun Dip."

"She's all about making the best time for the Marshmallow Run," Melli said, shaking her head.

"She should be concentrating on making the best peppermint sticks instead of a faster sled," Raina mumbled. "Princess Lolli asked Dash to make her two tall peppermint sticks for her new throne in Candy Castle. Did you all know that?" She looked around at her fairy friends. They all looked surprised.

Dash shot Raina a minty glare. "You don't have to talk about me as if I'm not here," she said. "Everything is under control."

The truth was, Dash felt very honored that the ruling fairy princess of Candy Kingdom had asked her to make the sticks for the new throne. When Princess Lolli asked fairies to do something, the fairies all did as she wished. Princess Lolli was a fair and true princess who was very generous and kind. She took good care of the Candy Fairies, and everyone in the valley loved her.

"I don't think Dash has been at Peppermint Grove at all this week," Cocoa said.

"That's not true!" Dash said, flying above her friends. "You don't know the first thing about growing peppermint sticks!"

Melli stepped forward. She didn't like when her friends argued. "Dash, we're just worried

 17

about you. It's not like you to miss Sun Dip."

"Or not do as Princess Lolli asks," Cocoa added. "Having peppermint sticks as part of the new throne in Candy Castle is a very big deal."

"That is pretty sweet," Berry said. She turned to Dash. "Have you been working on the peppermint sticks?"

"Yes," Dash said. She landed and planted her feet firmly on the ground.

"How's your new sled?" Melli asked. She sensed that Dash wanted to change the subject— and fast.

"It's *so mint*!" Dash replied with a grin on her face. "I think I have a chance to break Pep's record!" She sat down on Berry's blanket. "How sweet would that be? Today I tied his best time!" Reaching into Berry's basket, she picked a fruit chew and popped it in her mouth.

"Dash!" Berry scolded. "Those chews are not for eating. They're for my necklace that I'm making!" Berry held up a string of sparkled fruit jewels. Berry was very into accessories and never had enough jeweled fruit gems.

"Sorry," Dash said, shrugging. She licked her finger. "It was delicious."

"Did you really tie Pep's record?" Raina asked. "His record has been unbroken for years! No one has even come close to his time."

"Until this year, right, Dash?" Cocoa said.

Dash grinned. "It's all I can think about!"

Raina came over and sat next to Dash on the

blanket. "That's great, Dash," she said. "But you really need to figure out what's going on with your peppermint sticks. Princess Lolli is counting on you."

Melli and Cocoa shared a look. Berry kept her eyes on her fruit-chew necklace.

"You don't understand," Dash said. She looked toward the Frosted Mountains. "This race means everything to me."

"But you have lots of other responsibilities too," Raina said.

"Sorry I missed Sun Dip today," Dash said, getting up. She had just gotten there, but now all she wanted to do was leave. She couldn't stand the look of disappointment on Raina's face.

"Where are you going?" Melli asked.

"Home," Dash said. "I need to frost the tips of the sled again for tomorrow's run."

Raina sank down onto Berry's blanket. "You're not even going to check on the peppermint sticks?"

"I will," Dash assured her friend. "Don't worry."

"But I am worried," Raina said as Dash took off. "I'm very worried."

CHAPTER 3

Champion Race

The next morning, Dash flew out to the Frosted Mountains for another early-morning practice. As she flew over Peppermint Grove, she thought about what her friends had said to her. Maybe they were right. She really hadn't been spending as much time as she should have at the grove. She dipped down to see her peppermint sticks.

The strong, fresh, minty smell of the grove greeted Dash as she drew closer. This was a special place for her. She flew by the tiny mint candy bushes. They were budding new delicious-looking minty treats along the edge of the garden. Farther down the grove she spotted the peppermint sticks that were just starting to push out of the sugar soil.

Looking down the row of peppermint sticks, Dash realized that the sticks could have been bigger. She put her hand on one of the sprout sticks.

"This needs more mint," she said. She walked over to a small shed and got her mint can. She knew peppermint sticks needed lots of mint. Since some of these sticks were for Princess Lolli's new throne, she wanted them to be perfect. Even

though her friends thought she didn't care, she did. "I can race *and* raise peppermint sticks," she declared out loud.

While minting the soil, Dash was distracted. She couldn't stay too long in the grove. She had to keep up with her practice schedule. She sighed. If only her friends understood what breaking the Marshmallow Run record meant to her. Maybe then they wouldn't have given her such a hard time at Sun Dip.

Dash poured more white minty liquid into the ground. Then she gently pulled stray mint weeds from around the sticks and straightened the sugar fence around the grove.

There's no need to panic, Dash thought. She stood back and admired the peppermint stick crop.

Maybe she should spend more time here,

she thought, but she had to get going. A cool, refreshing breeze blew her blond hair and tickled her silver wings. She put her mint can back in the shed and headed toward the slopes. Time for another practice run!

Once Dash was on the slope, she double-checked her sled. Everything looked perfect. Just as she was getting ready to take her first run of the day, she sensed someone standing behind her. She turned to see a Mint Fairy. Dash squinted her eyes. And then her jaw dropped.

"Pep?" she said breathlessly. Her heart was beating extra fast.

The Mint Fairy walked over to Dash. "Yes, I'm Pep," he said. "You must be Dash. I've heard a lot about you."

Dash blushed. "You've . . . you've heard

about me?" she stammered. She could barely speak. Standing in front of her was one of the most famous fairies of all time. And certainly the fastest.

Pep laughed. His teeth were as white as the mint syrup Dash had poured around her peppermint sticks. And his bright green eyes twinkled like the sparks from a mint candy.

"Yes, of course I've heard about you," he said, smiling. "You are about to break my speed record, right?"

"I . . . I . . . Well, I hope to break your record," Dash spat out. She looked down at the packed powered sugar by her feet.

Nodding, Pep grinned. "Princess Lolli says you've got a good chance of beating the record," he told her. He winked. "I had to see you take a run for myself."

"I'm about to go now," Dash said.

"Would you like to race me?" Pep asked. He pulled a green mint sled out from behind a tree. "I'm up for a run. Would that be okay?"

All Dash could do was nod her head up and down. She was too excited to say anything! Racing against the most famous speed-racer fairy was a huge thrill. "Sure," Dash finally managed to say. She pulled her snow goggles down over her eyes and got set to race.

"Sweet!" Pep called out. He jumped on his sled and started to count down. "Three, two, one—GO!"

The two Mint Fairies raced down the slope. They were wing to wing for most of the ride, but when the marshmallow turn came, Pep sped ahead, and he won the race.

"Great race!" he said, lifting up his goggles. "Princess Lolli was right about you."

Dash took off her goggles. "Thank you," she said. "I've been practicing. I really want to beat your speed record. But I have big tracks to fill!"

Pep stood up. "You have an excellent chance," he told her. "I wasn't this fast when I was your age. You need to keep up the practicing. Those last turns through the marshmallow are pretty sticky. But with practice, you can do it."

Dash was so happy that Pep understood her wanting to break the record. "It's so great to talk to you," she said. "My friends don't really understand my racing. They keep after me about my candy duties. They don't get my need to race."

"Well, your friends are right too," Pep explained. He pulled his sled off the slope. "It's great to race, but your first responsibility is your candy crops."

"Have you been talking to my friend Raina?" Dash asked, smiling.

Pep shook his head. "No," he said, laughing. "But if she's after you about tending to your chores, then she is a good friend. A real champion is responsible." He wrapped the rope of his sled around his wrist. "Good luck, Dash. I'll be at the Marshmallow Run cheering you on." He flashed her a smile. "Remember, to be a champion, you

 31

have to think like a champion." He gave a wave and turned to leave.

"Thanks!" Dash called out. She was still in shock. As she watched Pep fly away, she thought about what he had told her. She squinted up at the sun. She realized a perfect way to make up with her friends. At Sun Dip tonight, she'd bring some special mint candies for her friends . . . along with an apology. A champion apology!

CHAPTER

4

Sugar Medal Bravery

Since Pep had suggested that Dash practice
the turns through Marshmallow Marsh, Dash
spent the rest of the day on that part of the
run, near the bottom of the slope. She weaved
in and out of the turns and tried to shave off
extra time. If Pep gave her advice, she was
going to take it!

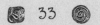

With time for one more full run, Dash was feeling confident. She climbed to the top of the slope for her final run of the day.

This time I can beat Pep's record, she thought. *I can be a champion! I know I can.*

She sat for a minute at the starting line and imagined crossing the finish line below in record time. She closed her eyes and took a deep breath.

Think like a champion! she told herself.

She knew this slope. She could break the old record!

With great sped, Dash went down the mountain. She cleared all the turns and jumps in good time. As she neared the Marshmallow Marsh, she steadied herself. She made a sharp left turn and then a quick right. Then she came around a turn, and something was in her way—something that was not supposed to be in the marsh. Dash steered her sled off the slope to avoid a crash and went straight into a sugar mound on the side of the trail.

"Who's there?" a voice grumbled loudly. "Who's that?"

Dash was startled from her near collision. She tried to catch her breath as she took off her goggles. Then she rubbed her eyes. Was she seeing clearly?

"Holy peppermint," she mumbled.

Standing in front of her was Mogu, the salty old troll from Black Licorice Swamp!

"Who are you?" Mogu growled. He stepped forward and stuck his huge nose down in Dash's face. He sniffed around her. "And what do we have here?" The troll peered down at the tasty sled made of the finest candy.

Dash had to think fast! She knew all about Mogu, who loved candy and stole Candy Fairy treats. He was a sour troll who was full of greed. When Mogu had tried to steal Cocoa's chocolate eggs, her friend had been very brave and strong. Cocoa had even gone to the Black Licorice Swamp on the other side of the Frosted Mountains to get the eggs back! Dash knew she had to be brave as well as clever to get out of this sticky situation. No way was that hungry troll going to get her sled as a snack!

"What do you want?" Dash asked, trying to be

strong. She stood up with her hands on her hips.

"Bah-haaaaaaa!" the troll laughed. "Such a tiny fairy. What are you doing here?"

Trying not to get fired up, Dash did her best to be calm. "The question is, what are *you* doing here," she said. "Marshmallow Marsh is far from Black Licorice Swamp."

Mogu sat down on a fallen tree stump, his big belly spilling over his short pants. He stuck his finger into a soft white mound of marshmallow. "I'm double-dipping today," he said, smirking. "I do love marshmallow." He licked his large thumb. Then he eyed Dash carefully. "But your sled looks very tasty too."

"My sled is not for eating!" Dash snapped.

Mogu laughed even louder. He stood up and waddled over to Dash. His white hair stuck out in a ring around his head. "Oh, I'm not sure about that," he said, licking his lips.

The last thing Dash wanted to do right before the Marshmallow Run was to hand over her new sled to Mogu.

Wrinkling his large nose, Mogu laughed again. "I don't really like mint, but I do enjoy licorice and sugar candies. And I see that is what your sled is made of." He leaned closer to the sled. "And frosted tips. Yum!"

Dash backed away. Mogu's stinky breath was awful!

"Let's make this easy," Mogu said, rubbing his big belly. "You just fly away and leave this for me to nibble on. A marshmallow-dipped sled!" He drummed his fingers on his large belly, and a wide grin appeared on his face.

"This is a very sweet surprise to find here in the marsh."

Staring up at Mogu, Dash couldn't help but notice that many of his teeth were missing. And the ones he had were rotten and black. The troll probably never brushed his teeth.

Dash shivered at the idea of the troll eating her hard work. She didn't want to hand over her sled. But what was she to do? Mogu was much bigger than she was, and much stronger. She looked down at her beautiful, fast sled. She couldn't stand the thought of the sled being a snack for Mogu.

Quickly, Dash tried to think of how Raina would advise her. Maybe she would tell her an encouraging story from the Fairy Code Book? And what about Berry, Cocoa, and Melli? They wouldn't be pushed around by a mean troll. After all, Cocoa even faced Mogu under the Black Licorice Bridge!

The time for sugar medal bravery is definitely now, Dash thought. But she was frozen with fear. The closer Mogu came to her, the more scared she became. What was she going to do? How could she save herself and her sled from Mogu?

CHAPTER 5

A Sticky Situation

Dash knew she was in a very sticky situation. Mogu was growing impatient, and she didn't want to give up her sled to the greedy troll. She could understand his appetite for her sled, but she couldn't let it happen. She had worked too hard on her sled all year to just hand it over to a hungry old troll! Her small silver wings fluttered as she tried to think of a plan.

"You're a Mint Fairy, aren't you?" Mogu said, sniffing around her. A sly grin spread across his face. "You almost smell good enough to eat."

Dash flew straight up in the air. Mogu reached up and grabbed her leg. "Where do you think you're going?" he grumbled. "I'm not letting you out of my sight!" He pulled Dash down and looked her in the eye. "What's a Mint Fairy like you doing in Marshmallow Marsh, anyway?"

"I'm practicing for the Marshmallow Run," Dash said, breaking free of the troll's grasp. "The race is in two weeks."

"Ah, silly fairy races," Mogu said, waving his hand. "A waste of good candy, that's what I say."

Dash didn't expect Mogu to understand about the race. She stood closer to her sled. She

43

didn't like how the troll was eyeing her prized possession.

"Candy is pretty sparse this time of year," he went on. "Maybe it's because you Mint Fairies are so small. I saw those tiny peppermint sticks in the grove. Those are yours? The tiny ones? Tiny candies for tiny fairies!" Mogu leaned his head back and hooted a large belly laugh. "Oh, I make myself chuckle," he said happily.

Trying to keep her cool, Dash took a deep breath. Her minty nature made her want to lash out at the mean troll, but she knew that wasn't the answer. Her mint candies were the sweetest in Sugar Valley. She had to keep focused on the task at hand. If she was going to outsmart this troll, she had to be clever and calm. Her only chance was to try to trick Mogu. She looked up to the Frosted Mountains, and suddenly she had an idea.

"You know," Dash said, "the Marshmallow Run is the hardest race in Sugar Valley. Only a few fairies take the challenge." She watched Mogu's reaction.

"Oh, please," Mogu said. He waved his chocolate-stained hand in front of his face. "I slide up and down the Frosted Mountains all the time. What's so hard about that?" He shook his head. "And I don't even use a silly sled," he added.

"Well," Dash said slowly, "how about you and I race?" She looked right into Mogu's dark, beady eyes.

"Me race you?" Mogu spat. "Oh, that's a good one," he bellowed. "*Baaa-haaaaa!!*" He hit his hand on his knee and continued to laugh. "You are no match for me. You're a tiny Mint Fairy."

So far he was taking the bait. Dash hoped that she could get the troll up on the slope. She stepped closer to the troll. "Yes, a race," Dash told him. "Just the two of us. And the winner gets to keep this sled." She stepped away from the sled, showing off all the delicious candy.

Mogu raised his bushy eyebrows.

"You could have this sled to race," Dash continued, and then sadly added, "or to eat."

Mogu tapped his thick finger on his chin. "Why should I race you when I can just eat the sled now?"

"I've been the fastest fairy on this slope for the past two years," Dash stated. "You don't think you can beat me?"

Mogu smiled. "Beat you?" the troll asked. "Why, you silly little fairy, of course I can beat you. I'm much bigger and faster." He gazed up at the trail zigzagging down the mountain. Then he looked over at Dash. "Nothing makes me happier than taking candy from a fairy. This will be fun. Let's race."

"Oh, it will be lots of fun," Dash mumbled.

Dash knew the slope was narrow and curvy. Without a sled the troll would have a hard time sliding down. But greed made Mogu answer quickly, and soon they were both up at the starting line.

"Are you ready?" Dash asked, looking over at the troll.

"Let's get this going already," Mogu spat out. "I'm hungry, and that sled of yours is looking

 47

delicious." He licked his lips as he looked at Dash's sled.

Dash cringed at the way Mogu was staring at her and her sled. There was no room for mistakes here. She had to keep steady and cross the finish line first. Everything was depending on this run.

"Three, two, one, GO!" Dash cried. She took a running start and jumped on her sled. As she rounded the first turn, Mogu was right next to her. He was laughing as he slid along on his large bottom.

"Oh, this is fun," he yelped as he slid along. "I can't wait for my snack at the bottom!"

Dash knew that there was a sharp turn up ahead, and that she had to reach that turn before Mogu. If she took the lead there, she'd be in

good shape to win. Mogu didn't realize the trail curved down the mountain. She was sure Mogu never went near the slope. He probably only slid down the open part of the mountain.

With great skill Dash took the turn, and the lead. Down the slope she went, gaining more and more speed. Glancing behind her, she saw Mogu struggling to stay on course.

"Ouch, ouch!" Mogu grunted as he squeezed himself through the narrow turn. "What kind of trail is this?"

Dash didn't bother to answer. She just kept going. Trolls cannot be trusted, and she wasn't about to wait around at the end to gloat about her win. She had to cross the finish line and get away as fast as she could. Trolls can't fly, and that was Dash's only way out. She just had to be far enough ahead of Mogu to be out of his reach.

The finish line was up ahead, and Dash could hear Mogu huffing and puffing behind her. On the final turn Dash picked up more speed and crossed the finish line. She had no idea if that run broke Pep's record or not. All that mattered was that she had beaten Mogu!

She lifted her sled up and waved at Mogu.

"Sorry, Mogu!" she called safely from the air. "You've been beaten by the tiniest fairy in Sugar Valley."

"Argh!" Mogu bellowed as he came to the finish line. He stayed on his back and looked up in the sky at Dash. "Salty sours!" he cried. He beat his fist on the ground.

Dash couldn't help but grin as she saw the

large troll lying on his back. She flew quickly back to Peppermint Grove. Now more than ever she had lots to prove. She wanted to break the speed record, but also prove Mogu wrong about her candy. She was about to make the best peppermint sticks Candy Kingdom had ever seen.

CHAPTER 6

Too Fast

The fresh scent of peppermint put a smile on Dash's face. She was so happy to be back in Peppermint Grove, far from Mogu. She still couldn't believe that she had challenged the troll to a race and won. Wait until her friends heard about her latest adventure!

Feeling lucky, Dash shined up her sled blades

with some fresh mint syrup. When her sled sparkled, she took the extra syrup over to the mint bushes at the far end of Peppermint Grove. She poured the white liquid on the branches. She took a deep breath, enjoying the magical moment of creating mint.

The tiny mint buds on the bushes glistened in the afternoon sun. Dash thought about how the crop of tiny mints would soon go to Candy Castle. At the castle fairies from all parts of the kingdom could use the flavoring in their own candies. Chocolate mint, sucking candies, and chewing gum all needed mint. Dash hummed happily as she tended to the her crops.

As she worked, Dash thought about what Mogu had said to her. "Salty old troll," Dash mumbled as she weaved her way through the peppermint sticks. Even though she was small, she could still make the best peppermint sticks in Sugar Valley. "You can be sure as sugar!" she grumbled.

A breeze blew her wings, and Dash noticed the sun getting closer to the top of the Frosted Mountains. She grabbed her bag and filled the sack with some fresh mint treats for her friends. She didn't want to be late for Sun Dip again today.

High above Red Licorice Lake, Dash spotted her friends. She was surprised to see all of them there. Was she late? Berry was never on time for Sun Dip. The Fruit Fairy was always the last one to arrive because she took her sweet time getting ready. Dash wondered what the special occasion was for them all to be there early.

"Hello!" Dash greeted the four fairies. They

were all huddled together and didn't see Dash flying in. "You are not going to believe what happened to me today!"

"Oh, Dash," Melli burst out, racing toward her. "Are you all right?"

"Maybe you want to sit down?" Raina asked.

Berry and Cocoa rushed to her side and spread a blanket on the red sugar sand.

"What's going on?" Dash asked, looking at her friends. "What's with the special treatment?"

The fairies all looked at one another. Raina put a hand on Dash's back. "We've heard about the race with Mogu."

"The sugar flies were all buzzing about the news," Berry told her.

"It must have been awful," Melli said, shuddering.

"Were you scared?" Raina asked.

"Wasn't he salty?" Cocoa added, wrinkling her nose.

Dash was a little disappointed that she didn't get to tell her friends about the race with Mogu herself. Those sugar flies were handy for getting messages to friends, but they could spread a story faster than mint spreads on chocolate.

"I'm fine," Dash said. She flew up fast from the blanket. "In fact, I'm great!"

Melli raised her eyebrows. She pushed Cocoa toward Dash.

"He's a tricky one, that Mogu," Cocoa said slowly. "Tell us what happened. Did he challenge you to a race?"

"No," Dash said. She put her hands on her hips. "Is that what the sugar flies told you?"

The fairies all nodded their heads at the same time.

"Yes," Raina said. "They said that he challenged you, but that you won."

"Well, at least the flies got that part of the story right," Dash said. She sat down on a nearby licorice rock. "He wanted to eat my sled. Can you believe that? I had to think fast and come up with a way to get away from him. Challenging him to a race was the only way."

"And the best way," Berry said with a smile. "You outsmarted Mogu! Well done, Dash."

"He said some mean things about mint candies and Mint Fairies," Dash reported. She looked down at her feet.

"He's just a bitter troll," Raina explained. "You shouldn't let his sour words get to you."

"That's right," Berry said. "He's just grumpy."

"Maybe if he didn't go around stealing candy and being so mean, he'd be happier," Melli added.

"Maybe," Dash said. She stood up. "But I want to prove him wrong. The peppermint sticks are going to be extra-tall this year. Princess Lolli wanted a special throne, and she's going to get a supercool minty one!"

"But what about the Marshmallow Run?" Cocoa asked.

"Oh, I can do that too," Dash said. "I have everything under control."

"We've heard that before," Raina said. She had a concerned look on her face. "We could help tend to the peppermint sticks or help you train for the race." She came up beside Dash and put her arm around her friend.

"I can do it," Dash told her. "I might be small, but I can handle this."

"No one said anything about you being small," Berry pointed out. "You just have a lot going on, and we want to help."

"You told me that I wasn't paying attention to my candy," Dash said. "And now I am. I thought you'd be happy." She picked up her bag. "I have to get back to the grove and then do some wing stretches. I have to be in the best shape possible if I am going to break that speed record." And with a wave, Dash was off.

Her four friends watched as Dash flew back to Peppermint Grove, worried that Dash was moving way too fast—even for a Mint Fairy.

CHAPTER 7

Magic Mint

Dash admired the tall and very thick peppermint sticks in Peppermint Grove. She grinned as she squinted up at the beautiful, strong candy. For two weeks Dash had carefully cared for the sticks. Early every morning she would arrive at Peppermint Grove and add more mint to the sugar soil. Her magic touch was working, and the sticks were growing beautifully.

Dash had also kept up with her practice schedule for the big race. In the afternoons she did her workouts and runs down the slope. Sticking to her training program was very important. Dash was one busy Mint Fairy.

Fluttering her silver wings, Dash flew over to the mint bushes along the edge of Peppermint Grove. She checked on the tiny white buds on the thin branches. The mints were ready to pick and send over to Candy Castle. Dash sighed. The Marshmallow Run was tomorrow. She really wanted to get two more practice runs in before Sun Dip today. Once the sun went down, she wouldn't be able to take her run down the slope. She'd have to pick the mints tomorrow. Hopefully as a new speed champion!

"Hello, Dash," a cheery voice called out.

Dash watched as Princess Lolli flew over to her. The beautiful fairy princess was wearing her candy-jeweled tiara and a bright pink dress. Her wings glistened in the winter sun as she settled down on the ground.

"I haven't seen you around this past week," the fairy princess said. She flashed Dash a sweet smile.

"I've been here," Dash explained, "and on the Frosted Mountain slope."

"Ah, yes," the princess said. Her strawberry-blond hair bounced around her shoulders. "Are you ready for the race?"

"Yes," Dash said. "I am."

"I heard about your run-in with Mogu," Princess Lolli said. She stared into Dash's blue

 65

eyes. "You were very brave. And your fast thinking to challenge him to a race was very smart."

"I had no choice," Dash told her. "I didn't want that salty troll to eat my sled!"

Princess Lolli laughed. "Well, your quick thinking is a match for your speed on the slope. Well done, Dash."

Dash blushed. She was happy that Princess Lolli had come by to see her. She flapped her wings excitedly. "I'd like to show you how the peppermints for your throne are growing," she said proudly.

Princess Lolli flew beside Dash and saw the tall sticks at the far end of the grove. "Dash, these are wonderful!" she exclaimed. "You have been working hard." She touched the beautiful candies

striped with red and white. "These will make my new throne extra-special. Thank you."

"I'm glad," Dash responded. "Now if I can only beat Pep's speed record. I want to be the fastest fairy in Sugar Valley!"

"There is more to the race than just speed," the princess said kindly. "Skill and quick thinking are needed to conquer that slope. I have a feeling that you are going to do very well this year, Dash. You've already proved yourself to be a real champion. I am very proud of you."

Dash's wings fluttered again. She felt like sailing high about the grove. It wasn't every day that Princess Lolli came to visit with so many compliments. Before Dash could respond, she saw her friends flying toward her.

"Hello, Princess Lolli," Raina called.

"We thought we'd come and see Dash," Berry told the princess.

As her friends flew down to Peppermint Grove, Dash smiled. She was glad to see them.

"I must get back to the castle," Princess Lolli said to all the fairies. "It was good to see you all," she added. "You are good friends to check on Dash. She's been very busy!"

"Byc!" Dash called after the fairy princess. "Thank you again for coming!"

"Wow." Melli sighed as the fairy princess flew off. "Princess Lolli just came by to see you?"

"She must have wanted to see how they are growing." Berry flew up to look over the crop of sticks. "And she must have been very happy to see these." She flew over to Dash. "The sticks are beautiful, Dash."

Raina put her arm around Dash. "I'm sorry we gave you a hard time," she said. "You really have come through for Princess Lolli."

Dash looked at her sparkly silver shoes. "Thanks, Raina," she said softly.

"And we don't want you to feel like you are doing this alone," Cocoa told her. "We know that the other Mint Fairies are busy with their crops, so we've come to help you." A wide grin spread across her face.

"Really?" Dash asked.

Berry laughed. "Sure as sugar!" she exclaimed. "Just tell us what to do. We're here to help!"

"Well," Dash said, walking down the grove's path, "if you are serious, I'd love some help picking the mint candies off the bushes. The candies are ready to go to Candy Castle, but

I wanted to get another practice run in before Sun Dip."

"Licking lollipops!" Berry shouted. "That's easy. We can do that in no time, right?" She turned to smile at her friends.

"Sure as sugar," they all said together.

With five fairies working, the bushes were picked clean quickly. When the baskets of fresh mints were lined up, Dash looked over the crop. "Wow," she said. "I never would have finished this so fast. Thanks for helping me out."

"Can we watch you take a practice run?" Melli asked. "I know you're superfast, but I'd love to get a little sneak peek."

"You bet!" Dash said. "I'd love for you all to come."

The fairy friends all flew to the slope on

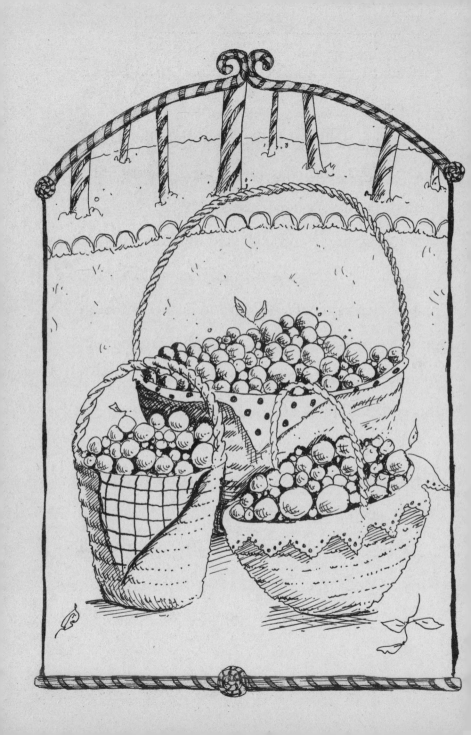

the near side of the Frosted Mountains.

"I'm glad that we don't have to fly *over* the mountain," Cocoa said.

Dash could tell that Cocoa was remembering when she had flown to Black Licorice Swamp to face Mogu. "Hopefully, Mogu will stay on his side of the mountain," Cocoa added.

"I bet he is still embarrassed to have lost the race with Dash," Berry added. She folded her arms over her chest. "Serves him right. He should have known better than to challenge Dash!"

"Now let's see how fast you are," Raina said, smiling at Dash.

Dash picked up her sled and headed for the top of the slope. With her friends by her side, there was nothing she couldn't do!

C H A P T E R

8

Race Day

The next morning Dash woke up extra-early. She didn't need an alarm to wake her. Today was race day!

Feeling good, Dash glided over Chocolate River. She took a deep breath. The delicious smell of the river filled the air, and Dash watched the rich brown chocolate rush below her. As much as she wanted to stop and have a quick snack, she kept on flying. She had to get to the Frosted Mountains.

Dash was focused on the race! She had checked on her peppermint sticks earlier that morning, and her candies were perfect. Thanks to her friends, she had gotten all her work done. Now she could concentrate on the race—and breaking the speed record.

When Dash saw the starting line banner, her heart began to beat faster. This was the most thrilling time of all!

Carefully, she iced her sled with fresh mint syrup, making the blades glisten in the morning sun. The cold air rushing around her carried the scent of all the winter candy from Sugar Valley. Dash's tummy rumbled. Again she was tempted to stop her work for a snack. But then she looked at her sled. She wanted to finish her task. Very soon the other racers would be there, and she wanted to be done with her race preparations before they arrived.

"Hey there!" Pep cried as he flew up beside Dash. "You are here nice and early!" He flashed her a toothy grin. "I used to love to get to races early too. Nothing beats the calm before the race, huh?"

Dash nodded. She knew that Pep understood. He held out his hand.

"I brought you some mint candies from my garden," he told her. "I hope you like them."

In Pep's hand were three red-, green-, and white-striped candies. They were beautiful. Dash took one and popped the candy into her

mouth. The candy melted away with a burst of mint in the middle. Her eyes grew wide as she tasted the minty flavor. "Yum!" she exclaimed. "These are extraordinary!"

"Thanks," Pep said shyly. "Now that I am not racing as much, I have more time to tend to my garden." He tossed his long hair out of his eyes. "But I wouldn't have traded all that time racing when I was younger. That was a very happy time for me."

"And for me, too!" Dash said, smiling. "I used to love watching you race. That's why I got into racing."

"Well, you are the favorite today," Pep told her. "And we'll all be cheering for you. Remember, take the course slow around that final bend. The marshmallow gets sticky down there."

Dash nodded. She knew just the area that Pep was talking about. "I will," she said. "And thanks for the candy."

As Pep walked away, Dash saw her friends gathered in tight huddle. They came rushing up to her.

"Lickin' lollipops!" Berry exclaimed. "Was that really Pep? He is even sweeter-looking close up! I've only gotten glimpses of him from the sidelines."

"He is supersweet," Dash said, watching him fly off. "He has been giving me good advice."

Cocoa flapped her wings. "That's nice of him. You could break his record today and he still wants to help you out?"

Dash stood back to admire her polished sled. "Well, he'll always hold that record," she said.

"He's the first ever to have gone that fast. I just hope I can prove myself today."

"I think you've already proved yourself," Raina said kindly. "What Mint Fairy ever challenged Mogu to a race and won?"

"While that fairy was growing candy for a royal throne," Cocoa added.

"And won the Marshmallow Run two years in a row," Melli chimed in.

"Soon to be three years in a row," Berry said, laughing.

Dash smiled at her friends. "Thanks," she said. "It means a lot to me to have you here."

"We'll always be here for you," Raina said. She flew over to Dash and gave her a tight squeeze.

Dash made her way to the starting line. There were more racers than ever before. She looked down the lineup of fairies. There were not only Mint Fairies, but all kinds of fairies from around the kingdom. Dash felt nervous. But then she felt Raina's hand on her arm and saw her friends smiling at her. She placed her goggles over her eyes. She was ready to race!

The caramel horn sounded and the race began! Dash quickly took the lead. She knew the race route well. She held the sled's crossbar tightly and steered down the slope. As she took the turn toward Marshmallow Marsh, she checked behind her. No one was there! She was doing great on time. She hunched down low and tried to gain more speed.

On the next turn Dash felt a bump and then noticed that the left blade on her sled was wobbling. She had no choice but to slow the sled

 81

down and pull over to the side. She jumped off to examine the sled. Quickly, she saw the problem.

One of the licorice screws that attached the blade to the sled was missing! Dash looked around on the slope for the sticky peg but couldn't spot it anywhere. How could she continue on? Her sled started to wobble more and more. How could she beat the time—or win—with a broken sled? What was she going to do?

CHAPTER 9

A Little Mint

Dash shook her head. Of all the days for a licorice screw to fall out of her sled! This was the most important race! The Marshmallow Run was only once a year. And this was supposed to be her year to break the record. She kicked the ground with her silver boot. Powdered sugar flew all around. This was not how she thought the race would turn out.

What would Pep do? Dash wondered. As she stared at her sled, she remembered that Pep had skidded off the slope in one race. His sled hit a piece of rock candy. He damaged his sled very badly, and he wasn't able to finish the race.

Dash looked over at her sled and thought again. Riding on a broken sled was very dangerous. Her only chance was to fix the sled. And fast.

I built this sled, she thought. *I can fix it!*

Up on the mountain Dash saw the other racers coming down the slope. She had the lead now, but if she couldn't fix her sled quickly . . .

Dash flapped her wings nervously. The cold mountain air was making her shiver. Down the mountain Dash could see a crowd gathering at the finish line. Pep was waiting for her there—and so were her friends. Knowing that she wasn't alone made her feel stronger and gave her a burst of energy.

She put her hands on her hips. In her side pocket she felt a bottle of mint syrup from her morning's work in Peppermint Grove. Holding up the bottle, she thought about how helpful her friends had been the other day. They had given her a hard time earlier, but in the end they were there for her. Just like this mint!

"Holy peppermint!" Dash cried. "That's the answer!" She smiled. "It's worth a try!" she exclaimed. The bright white liquid seemed to glow in the sunlight. She poured the sticky liquid into the hole and stuck the blade back. "Cool

Mint!" Dash said with a smile on her face. The sticky mint held the blade in place!

"Dash! Are you okay?" Raina asked, suddenly appearing by her side. She turned to the other fairies behind her. "See!" she said. "I knew something was wrong."

"What happened?" Cocoa asked. She flew down and put her hand on Dash's shoulder.

Berry and Melli flew down next to Dash. They all had the same worried expression.

"A licorice screw fell out of my sled," Dash said as she flipped it back over. She looked around at her friends' worried expressions. "But I've solved the problem," she said. "Nothing that a little mint couldn't fix!" She tossed Cocoa the bottle of mint. Then she took a running leap and jumped back on her sled.

"Go, Dash!" Cocoa shouted.

"The others are coming," Melli said nervously.

"Don't worry, you have a good lead," Raina said to Dash. She pointed up the mountain to the other racers. "Go! Go! Go!"

"You can do it, Dash!" Berry cheered. "You can make up the time."

"Thanks," Dash said, looking back at her friends. She was glad they had come by to find her. Hearing their encouraging words made her feel stronger. She could still win and beat Pep's time . . . that is, if she got moving! She looked overhead as her friends flew back to the finish line.

She flapped her wings to gain a little more speed. Up ahead was the stickiest part of the race—the beginning of Marshmallow Marsh.

Taking a deep breath, Dash held on to the bar of the sled. She took the curves quickly, never losing her balance or breaking her speed. She could hear the other racers coming up behind her, but she kept her focus. Up ahead was the finish line. A large crowd of fairies was gathered, and they were cheering loudly.

"Go, Dash!"

"Way to go!"

Dash heard all the cheers, but she didn't look up from the slope. Marshmallow Marsh was gooey, and she had to concentrate. If she veered off the course, she could get stuck in the sticky white marshmallow.

The cheers were getting louder. Dash saw

the rainbow banner of lollipops . . . the finish line! She huddled down low on the sled to pick up speed.

"Dash the Mint Fairy is the first to cross the finish line!" the announcer exclaimed.

There was a roar of applause from the crowd. Dash threw back her head and let out a whoop! In a flash, her friends were around her, giving her a hug. She won!

CHAPTER
10

So Mint

W hat was my time?" Dash asked. She couldn't see the giant marshmallow clock. There were too many people crowded around her. Her wings were being smushed, and she couldn't fly up to see her official race time. Her heart was beating so fast.

Cocoa took a step back and made room for

Dash to fly up high to see the clock.

Dash's wings drooped, and she sank back down to the ground. "I didn't break the speed record," she reported sadly.

"But you are still the winner of the race!" Raina said, trying to cheer her friend up.

"That's right, Dash," Cocoa said. "You're *so mint*!" She smiled at her friend. "You still came in first!"

Dash nodded, but she still couldn't help but feel disappointed. She had worked so hard to get the fastest time. "Has anyone seen Pep?" she asked her friends. "Maybe he is really disappointed in me," Dash said, looking down at the ground.

"How could he be disappointed in you?" Raina asked. "You were extraordinary out there

 93

on the slopes. Many other fairies would have given up or wouldn't have had the strength to finish at all."

"And you didn't just finish," Berry pointed out, "you won!"

"*So mint*," Pep said from behind Berry. He stepped forward with a dazzling smile. "Dash, you made me proud."

"But I didn't break the record," Dash mumbled.

Pep came over to her and put his arm around her. "Not this time, but there's always next year. Plus, it took more skill and bravery to run the race you just did. Remember my race when I skidded off the slope? I didn't have the courage or smarts to do what you did out there today."

Dash felt her cheeks grow redder than the stripes of a peppermint stick!

"I need to thank my friends for making me feel brave," Dash said. She turned to smile at them. "They helped me the most."

"I can see that," Pep said. "You are very lucky."

Before Dash could say another word, Princess Lolli was by her side. "Dash, I heard what happened on the slope. I am very proud of you. You acted wisely and quickly. And you are by far one of the fastest Mint Fairies I have ever seen! Even with your delay, you still came in first. You should be very proud of yourself."

"Thank you," Dash said, bowing her head.

"Come," Princess Lolli said. She held out her hand to Dash. "We are about to have the award ceremony."

Dash took Princess Lolli's hand and flew up to the stage. A crowd of fairies surrounded the stage at the far end of Marshmallow Marsh. A special fruit leather carpet was laid down on the ground for the crowd to stand on and watch.

"I proudly award Dash the Mint Fairy the chocolate marshmallow trophy," Princess Lolli told the crowd.

Flying up to get her award, Dash smiled. Even though she had won two other times, winning this race seemed much sweeter. She proudly took the trophy that was nearly as tall as she was! Then she went back to stand with her friends.

"As many of you know," Princess Lolli continued, "Dash was trying to break the speed record that Pep set a few years ago."

Dash wanted to fly off and hide beneath her wings. She felt everyone in the kingdom staring at her. She was so embarrassed!

"Due to an unexpected problem on the slope today, Dash was not able to break that record," Princess Lolli continued on.

"Why is she telling everyone that?" Dash whispered to Raina.

"Shhh," Raina said. "Let's see what she's going to say."

"What Dash doesn't know is that she broke another record today," Princess Lolli declared. She smiled kindly at the tiny Mint Fairy and waved her back onto the stage. "Dash, no one has ever won three races in a row. You have set a new record!"

Pep squeezed Dash's shoulders from behind. "I never won three races in a row," Pep said. "When my sled sped off the slope, I wasn't able to think as fast and fix my sled. I lost that year."

He gave Dash a little push. "Go up and get your prize. You deserve it."

"And now you'll be listed in the Fairy Code Book!" Raina exclaimed. "All the record holders are in there."

"*Choc-o-rific*, Dash!" Cocoa shouted.

Berry and Melli hugged Dash and then clapped as their friend flew back up to the stage.

"Well done," Princess Lolli told Dash. She handed her a scroll and a beautifully carved piece of wintergreen mint with gold sugar writing. "We're all proud of you."

"Thank you," Dash said. Her feet lifted off the ground as she fluttered her wings happily.

All her friends gathered around her and gave her a hug.

"Come on," Cocoa said, pulling Dash's hand. "Everyone is heading to Peppermint Grove."

"There's more celebrating to be done!" Berry cheered. She twirled around in her new dress and touched her sparkly fruit-chew barrettes. "Dash, you can't miss the peppermint stick presentation."

In the center of Peppermint Grove, Dash had placed her four peppermint sticks for the fairy princess. The sticks were thick and very tall. Perfect for a new throne!

Princess Lolli was thrilled at the size and color of the sticks. "What a perfect treat," she said. "Thank you, Dash. These are the sticks of a true champion. I will always think of that when I sit on my new throne." She reached out to hug Dash.

The rest of the fairies were busy celebrating.

There was music, and there were lots of mint candies around for the fairies to eat. And Cocoa brought a barrel of dark chocolate chips with fresh white sprinkles for everyone. Berry was right—it was a delicious celebration.

Dash plucked a fresh candy cane from the garden. The candy was sweet and refreshing. A smile spread across her face.

Winter was one of the most magical times in Sugar Valley. And winning was definitely sweeter with good friends and some cool mint.

Magic Hearts

For Danielle, my sweet niece!

CHAPTER
1

A New Fairy Friend

What do you think?" Berry held up a string of colorful fruit chews. The Fruit Fairy enjoyed making delicious fruit candies, but she also loved making jewelry. The more sparkle the better! Berry loved anything and everything to do with fashion.

"Berry," Raina said. She had a worried look

on her face. The Gummy Fairy was filling up a bottle of cherry syrup for the trees in Gummy Forest. She had come to Fruit Chew Meadow for flavoring for the red gumdrop trees—and to visit Berry. But instead of finding Berry working on her fruit candies, her friend was making a necklace!

"Those are round chews," Raina said. "Where are the hearts?"

Berry shrugged. "These round fruit chews are just so pretty," she said with a heavy sigh. She held up the colorful strand again and admired the rainbow pattern she had made. "I just had to make a necklace with them!" She carefully knotted the end of the string. Then she put on a special caramel clasp that Melli, her Caramel Fairy friend, had made for her. Berry placed the finished necklace around her neck. She proudly spread her pink wings as she showed off her newest creation.

"Berry, Heart Day is coming up," Raina said gently. After she put the cap on the syrup bottle, she looked up at her friend. "Everyone in Sugar Valley is busy making candy hearts. And you're stringing round chews! You don't want to disappoint Princess Lolli, do you?"

Berry dragged her foot along the ground. There was a layer of powdered sugar that had fallen during the evening. It was a cold winter's day in Sugar Valley. The cool winds were blowing, and there was a chill in the air. "Sweet strawberries!" Berry exclaimed. "I would never want to upset Princess Lolli!"

Princess Lolli was the ruling fairy princess of Candy Kingdom. She was a caring and gentle fairy, and always treated the fairies very well. All the fairies loved her and wanted to please her. The sweet princess's favorite shape was a heart, so every fairy in the kingdom made special candy hearts from flavors found all over Sugar Valley. There were chocolate, gummy, mint, caramel, and fruit heart candies for Princess Lolli and the fairies to enjoy. Heart Day was a happy day, filled with good cheer—and delicious candy.

"I still have time to make something for Princess Lolli," Berry said. "Last year she loved my red fruit hearts, remember? I put a fruit surprise in each one and sprinkled them with red sugar."

Raina nodded. "Yes, and you spent weeks making those. Don't forget that Heart Day is next week."

"I will start on something today," Berry declared.

At that moment another Fruit Fairy flew up to the friends. Berry had just met her the other day. Her name was Fruli, and she was new to Sugar Valley. She had long blond hair, and today she was wearing the most beautiful dress

Berry had ever seen. There were tiny purple and pink candies sewn along the collar and cuffs that sparkled in the sun. Over her dress was a soft cape made of pink-and-white cotton candy. The fairy soared down next to them with her pale pink wings.

"Hi," Raina said. "You must be new here."

"This is Fruli," Berry said, introducing Raina to the newest Fruit Fairy. "She's from Meringue Island."

"Welcome to Sugar Valley," Raina said. "I've never been to Meringue Island, but I've read about the place. There's a story in the Fairy Code Book about the majestic Meringue Mountains. I've heard the island is beautiful and is the center of fashion." She smiled at Berry. "Berry loves fashion too."

Berry blushed. "Raina loves to read," she quickly explained. "She's memorized the Fairy Code Book."

Raina laughed. "Well, I do like to read. What about you, Fruli?"

"Yes, I like to read," she said very softly. She looked down at her white boots. Her response was so quiet that Berry and Raina could barely hear her.

"I love your cape," Raina said tentatively, eyeing the fabric and design. "Is that from Meringue Island?"

Fruli nodded. "Yes," she said. She didn't raise her eyes from the ground. "I'm sorry to interrupt."

Again, her voice was so low and soft, Berry and Raina could barely hear her.

"I just came to collect a couple of fruit chews for Princess Lolli," Fruli said.

"Well, you came to the right place," Raina said, smiling. She gave Berry a little push forward. She wondered why her friend was being so quiet around this new fairy. Usually, Berry was very outgoing and not shy at all. "Berry grows the best fruit chews on this side of the Frosted Mountains." She put her arm around her friend.

"Raina," Berry mumbled, feeling embarrassed. She smoothed her dress with her hands and noticed a big cherry syrup stain on the front.

Oh no, Berry thought. *What a big mess! Fruli has the nicest clothes. And look at me!*

"These chews?" Fruli asked, pointing.

"Yes," Berry said. "Please take anything you want."

Fruli took a few candies and put them in a white chocolate weave bag. "Thank you," she said.

Before Berry or Raina could say a word, she flew off.

"She was so shy!" Raina exclaimed.

"Did you see her clothes?" Berry asked. "She has the nicest outfits. I have *got* to get moving on making a new dress for Heart Day."

"Berry—," Raina started to say.

"I know," Berry said, holding up her hand. "I will make the heart candies, but I also need to find something new to wear to Candy Castle for Heart Day."

Berry flew off in a hurry, leaving Raina standing in Fruit Chew Meadow alone. Raina was worried. When Berry got an idea stuck in her head, sometimes things got a little sticky.

CHAPTER 2

Wild Cherry

Berry sat in front of two large pieces of fruit-dyed fabric. Bright pinks and reds were swirled around the material in large circles. Berry had been saving the material for something special, and a new outfit for Heart Day was the perfect occasion!

For a week she had tried drawing designs

for a new dress. Normally, designing a dress was fun and exciting for her. But this time nothing seemed right. To make things a little more sour, none of her friends understood her passion for fashion. Raina kept asking about heart candies, and her other friends did not seem interested in her dress designs. Berry sighed as she picked up the chalk to sketch out the dress form.

"I wish I could go to Meringue Island," she mumbled to herself. Even though the material in her hand was silky smooth, she was still feeling unsure. If only she could fly to the small, exclusive Meringue Island, she could buy a bunch of stylish new outfits. Meringue Island was known for high fashion and tons of cool accessories. Fruli probably thought all the fairies in Sugar Valley dressed terribly. Berry looked down at her red shiny dress. She used to love this one, but after seeing Fruli's dresses, she felt sloppy and very plain.

Berry didn't want to think about the beautiful dress that Fruli would be wearing on Heart Day. Thinking of what Fruli would wear made her face scrunch up like she had eaten a sour lemon ball.

I'll show her that Sugar Valley fairies know fashion and accessories too! Berry thought. She smoothed out the fabric and took out her scissors.

Her new dress was going to be the nicest one she'd ever made!

With thin caramel thread, Berry skillfully sewed up the dress. For extra sparkle, she added some of her new fruit chews around the collar.

She stood back and admired the dress. A smile spread across her face.

"Straight from the runways of Meringue Island," she said, pretending to be an announcer. "We are proud to carry the designs of Berry the Fruit Fairy!"

Berry slipped into the dress and spun around. Giggling, she felt so happy and glamorous. All her hard work had paid off.

Looking up at the sky, Berry noted the sun getting closer to the Frosted Mountains. Once the sun hit the top, Sun Dip would begin. At the end of the day her fairy friends gathered on the shores of Red Licorice Lake. They shared stories and snacked on candy. Usually, Berry was the last fairy to arrive.

Maybe today I'll surprise them, she thought. *I can be the first one there!*

She checked herself in the mirror and then flew out over the valley to Red Licorice Lake.

As she flew, Berry wished she had candy hearts for Princess Lolli. If the candies were finished, she'd have more time to make accessories for her new outfit. Berry smiled to herself. After all, accessories were the key to fashion! Maybe she could add a shawl, or even a cape? She had read all the fashion magazines and flipped through this season's catalogs. She could come up with something fabulous!

Seeing the tall spirals of Candy Castle off in the distance made Berry's heart sink. She realized she couldn't go to Heart Day empty-handed! She desperately needed a heart-shaped candy for the fairy princess.

Just then something red caught her eye. Down by the shores of Chocolate River there was something red and shiny glistening in the sun. Curious, Berry flew down to check out what was there. As she got closer, she saw that there was a small vine growing in the brown sugar sand.

"How odd," Berry said. Usually, there were some chocolate flowers growing there, but this vine looked different. She peered down closely at the plant. Berry couldn't believe her eyes! On the vine were tiny red hearts!

"Licking lollipops!" she cried out.

She reached down and plucked one of the hearts off the tiny vine.

Berry couldn't believe her luck. She was just wishing for candy hearts, and then they appeared!

These must be magic hearts, she thought.

Holding the heart in her hand, Berry examined the tiny candy. The rosy red color made her believe that these were cherry flavored. A bonus that cherry was one of Princess Lolli's favorite flavors. Carefully, Berry picked the hearts off the vine and placed them in her basket. Now she had something for Heart Day—and had time to finish her outfit!

After her basket was full, Berry flew over to Red Licorice Lake. It was the perfect day for her to be early for Sun Dip. She had lots to share with her friends today. She had news of her latest dress design, and magic heart candies for Princess Lolli. Maybe today wasn't so sour after all! Sweet wild cherry magic hearts just saved the day.

CHAPTER

3

Sweet Hearts

Berry spread her blanket on the red sugar sand and waited for her friends to arrive. The sun was just hitting the white tips of the mountains, and she knew that soon her friends would be there.

Dash the Mint Fairy was the first to arrive. Dash was the smallest Mint Fairy in the kingdom, but she had the biggest appetite!

"Berry, what are you doing here so early?" Dash cried as she swept down to the ground. She eyed Berry's new outfit. "You look fantastic. Is that a new dress?"

Smiling, Berry nodded. "I just made it!" she exclaimed.

"So mint!" Dash said. "I love the colors."

Cocoa the Chocolate Fairy and Melli the Caramel Fairy flew up next.

"Is this a special Sun Dip?" Melli asked. She looked Berry up and down. "You are wearing such a fancy dress."

"Hot chocolate! Where did you get that?" Cocoa asked, amazed. "It's fabulous."

Berry was enjoying all her friends' reactions to her new outfit. She stood up and spun in a circle. "It is pretty, don't you think?"

"I do," Melli said. "But I didn't get a sugar fly message about dressing up for tonight."

Berry laughed. "I just wanted to show you all my new outfit for Heart Day," she said.

"Yum!" Dash cheered. "I can't wait for Heart Day. I made the most delicious mint hearts, and Cocoa has promised to dip them in dark chocolate for me."

"That's right," Cocoa added. "Mint and chocolate hearts are an excellent combination." The two friends high-fived.

Dash turned to Melli. She knew that Melli and Cocoa often worked together, but this year Melli wanted to work on her own heart candies. "What did you make?"

A smile appeared on Melli's face. She dipped

her hand in her basket and pulled out a delicate heart.

"Is that caramel?" Dash asked, coming closer. She looked at the fragile heart in Melli's hand. The dark caramel looked like fine thread, but the candy was hard and didn't break when she touched it.

"That looks like imported lace!" Berry said. She leaned in to get a better look. "Melli, that is beautiful work."

"How long did that take you to make?" Dash asked.

Cocoa put her arm around Melli. "I told you these hearts were truly special," she told her.

Melli grinned. "Thank you," she said. "I've been working on these candies for weeks. I just hope Princess Lolli likes them."

"She's going to love those hearts," Dash told her. Then she licked her lips. "Maybe I should just try one to make sure they taste okay?"

"Dash!" Melli scolded. But then she started to laugh. "I knew you'd say that, so I brought some extra for tonight."

Dash's face brightened. "Ah, you are a good friend, Melli," she replied. Then she took a bite of the caramel heart. "Sweetheart, that is a *sweet heart*!" she said, laughing.

"Thank you," Melli said, and blushed.

"Wow, Berry!" Raina cried as she swooped down to her friends. "You have been working hard." She settled herself down on the blanket that Berry had spread out for the fairies. "The dress is beautiful. A true original."

Berry was bursting with pride.

 129

"If you had time to make that dress, you must have finished your candy, right?" Raina asked.

Berry looked over at Raina. She had expected that Raina would say something like that. And she was ready! "Actually, I do have my heart candy," she replied. She placed her basket of tiny red hearts in the center of her blanket. Though she had not worked as hard on her candy as Melli, Berry was still excited to show off the new candy.

The fairies all moved closer to the basket.

"*So mint*!" Dash shouted. "Berry, you *do* have hearts for Princess Lolli!" She turned to look at Raina. "And you were worried about Berry. See, I told you she'd come through."

Berry hugged Dash. "Thanks, Dash," she said.

"You managed to make a dress and these

candies?" Melli asked. She peered into the basket. "That's very impressive, Berry."

Cocoa shook her head. "It takes me weeks to get chocolate hearts right," she said. "Hearts are the hardest shapes to make!"

"Well," Berry said. She was about to confess that she had found the candy, but then she held back.

Raina fluttered her wings. She peered down at the red candies. "There's something very familiar about these hearts," she said. She took the Fairy Code Book out of her bag. She placed the thick volume on the ground and quickly flipped through the pages. "I know I've seen those candies before." She didn't look up at her friends. She continued to thumb through the pages.

Dash reached over to the basket. "What flavor are they, Berry?"

"Cherry, of course," Berry stated proudly. "Princess Lolli's favorite flavor!"

Dash popped a heart in her mouth. Her blue eyes grew wide, and her wings flapped so fast she shot straight up in the air. "Holy peppermint!" she cried.

"What's wrong?" Cocoa exclaimed, reaching up to grab Dash. "Are you all right?"

"Those are not sweet hearts!" she said, scrunching up her face. "Those are sour wild cherry hearts!"

All the fairies gasped. Berry's hands flew to her mouth. Her not-so-sweet hearts had suddenly made Sun Dip very sour.

C H A P T E R

4

Sour Surprise

Berry shuddered. She felt awful about lying to her friends. She didn't know much about sour candy. She only knew that some was grown in Sour Orchard. While many fairies enjoyed the sweet-and-sour crops from the orchard at the far end of Sugar Valley, Berry did not. She preferred the sweet, fruity flavors of her own candy.

"Are you okay?" Berry asked Dash. She went over to her and put her hand on her friend's back. Dash's silver wings fluttered and brushed Berry's hand.

"Yes," Dash said. "I'm fine. I like those sour candies." She licked her fingers.

"Leave it to Dash to like just about any candy!" Cocoa said, giggling. "Even the most sour."

Dash shrugged her shoulders and looked over at Berry. "I just wasn't expecting that from a candy *you* grew," she said. "Those hearts looked so sweet and delicious."

Berry hung her head. "Well, I didn't grow these," she admitted, looking down at the ground. "I picked them from the bank of Chocolate River. They were beautiful—and heart-shaped."

 134

"So you have no idea where these came from?" Melli asked. Her hand flew to her gaping mouth. "You don't know what these candies are made of?"

"And you didn't even test them first?" Cocoa added, amazed. "What happens if the hearts are poisonous or something horrible!"

"Cocoa!" Melli said. She never liked when her friends argued. She could tell that Cocoa's comment was making Berry upset. She turned her attention to Dash. "She looks the same. Are you feeling okay?"

"Stop looking at me like that!" Dash cried. "The hearts were good." She reached out toward Berry's basket.

"Dash!" all the fairies said at the same time.

Berry grabbed her basket away.

 135

"Cool down," Dash said. She sat on the ground next to Raina.

Suddenly Raina gasped. While her friends had been talking, she had been carefully reading the Fairy Code Book. "I knew those heart candies looked familiar," she said. She pointed to a picture at the bottom of the page. "Look here," she instructed.

The fairy friends all leaned over the book. There was a picture of the heart candies. And next to the picture was a drawing of Lemona, a Sour Orchard Fairy.

"Are they dangerous?" Cocoa asked.

"Don't be so dark," Melli said. She kneeled down closer to the book.

"Maybe they are magic because they simply

appear when someone wishes for heart candies?" Berry said hopefully.

"Or maybe the hearts will make me fly faster down the mountain on my sled!" Dash exclaimed. She flew up in the air and did a high dive back down to the ground. "Wouldn't that be *so mint?*"

Berry knew that speeding down the Frosted Mountain trails was one of Dash's favorite things to do. Nothing would make her Mint Fairy friend happier than being the fastest fairy in the valley. She was already the smallest—and one of the fastest. While Dash flew in circles up in the air, Berry studied the Fairy Code Book. Her eyes grew wide as she read the rest of the information. She peered back up at Dash.

Sweet syrup! she thought. *What a sticky mess!*

 138

Why hadn't she tested the candies? How could she have been so lazy? One of the first rules of making candy was that every fairy had to know the source of the ingredients. Berry's wings drooped lower to the ground as she read more about the magic hearts.

Dash came down and stood next to Berry's blanket. Berry wanted to tell her how sorry she was for what she had done. She had never meant to hurt Dash. She turned to her friend. But when Berry saw what was in front of her, she was speechless. Her mouth gaped open, and her eyes didn't budge from the sight in front of her.

"Why is everyone looking at me like that?" Dash asked. She saw the worried expressions on the faces in front of her.

 139

The Fairy Code Book had used the words "might happen" to describe the effects of the candy. But something was *definitely* happening to Dash!

Dash's skin was bright yellow!

CHAPTER 5

A Big Heart

O h, Dash!" Berry cried out. She couldn't bear to see her friend a bright yellow color!

It was not often that fairies changed colors. Berry could think of one other time that had happened. A few years ago many of the fairies got the sugar flu. The virus was awful. Fairies couldn't fly or make any candy, and several fairies turned scarlet from the high fever. Princess Lolli set up stations in the castle for the sick fairies. Luckily, Berry, Melli, and Cocoa hadn't gotten the flu. But Dash and Raina had. Berry sighed. At least they were able to take medicine and get better. There were no viruses or germs to blame here.

This was all Berry's fault.

No one said anything. Dash fluttered her wings.

"Why is everyone staring at me?" she snapped.

"Well, she's certainly acting like the same old Dash," Cocoa said, watching the Mint Fairy.

"She doesn't look affected at all," Melli added. She shook her head in disbelief. "Except for the fact that she is now yellow."

"Yellow?" Dash screeched. "I'm yellow? As in

 143

lemon frosting and lemon drops?" She looked down at her body and screamed.

Berry reached into her bag and gave Dash a small compact mirror. "Lemon yellow," Berry said sadly. "Take a look in the mirror. You'll see the color is all over your face."

Dash opened the candy-jeweled case and peered into the mirror. "A yellow Mint Fairy?" she cried. She snapped the mirror shut. Panicked, Dash grabbed Raina's hand. "Please tell me this will go away." When there was no reply from Raina, Dash took a deep breath. "Well, is there any medicine I can take? There must be something to make this go away, right?" She examined her yellow arms and hands.

Raina flipped through some more pages of the Fairy Code Book. "I can't find anything

more here in the book," she said. "It's odd. The book only mentions a slight change of coloring. I wonder why the bright yellow?"

"If Raina doesn't know the answer, this must be bad," Cocoa whispered to Melli.

"There is no medicine for magic spells," Melli said. "Oh, Dash . . ."

"Melli is right," Raina added. "We'll need to figure out the magic before you can get better."

"Why yellow?" Dash balked. "Blech!"

"There's only one way to fix this," Berry said. She stood up. "I have to go ask Lemona about her candy. If she's the fairy who made the candy, she'll know the answer to this riddle."

"What?" Dash said. "You, Berry the sweet and beautiful Fruit Fairy, want to venture into Sour Orchard?"

Dash might have been mocking Berry, but there was truth to what she was saying. Berry enjoyed fine fashions and sparkly accessories and was not one for flying out of her comfortable sweet spots.

"What if Lemona is as sour as her candy?" Melli asked.

"Oh, how awful," Cocoa said. "Do you think she could be like Mogu?"

"Mogu is a salty old troll who lives in Black Licorice Swamp," Raina said, shaking her head. "Lemona is one of us, a Candy Fairy."

"A Candy Fairy who lives in Sour Orchard," Melli mumbled.

Dash flew around in circles. "This color can't last, can it?" she asked. When no one answered, Dash landed and hung her head.

"Holy peppermint," she whispered. "I'll be the joke of Sugar Valley."

Berry took Dash's hand. "Don't get upset, Dash," she said. "I am going to find a way to help you. I promise."

"You'd really go to Sour Orchard for me?" Dash asked. She peered up at Berry.

"I should never have neglected my candy duties," Berry admitted. She folded her knees up to her chest. "If I hadn't been so concerned about making a new dress, then I would have made time to grow my own candy hearts for Heart Day." She gazed at Dash. "And I should have told the truth about those heart candies. Will you forgive me?"

"I'm not mad," Dash said. "I understand." She stuck her hand in her backpack. "Here, take these peppermint candies. It's getting dark and you might need light in Sour Orchard."

"Thank you," Berry told her. Dash might have been small, but she had the biggest heart of all. "I am truly sorry."

Suddenly Raina shot up from her spot on the blanket. "Oh, I found something more here," she said. She pointed to a section in the Fairy Code Book.

"I don't think I've ever been so grateful for that book," Dash said. She moved closer to Raina.

"When visiting Sour Orchard," Raina began to read, "you should bring a gift to a Sour Orchard Fairy. Sour Orchard Fairies are fond of fresh fruit blossoms."

Berry smiled. "I know where to get some

fresh and delicious orange blossoms!"

Even though it was winter in Sugar Valley, the orange trees were blossoming. The magic orange trees produced tangy and sweet candy fruit all year. Fruit Fairies took the oranges and dipped the slices into chocolate or made sweet fruit nectar for candies throughout the valley. Just that morning Berry had flown by the orange trees along the edge of Fruit Chew Meadow. Their sweet citrus smell always made her smile. It seemed even Sour Orchard Fairies enjoyed the fresh scents and tastes of the blossoms.

"Going to Sour Orchard with something to make Lemona happy will make the journey easier," Berry said.

"I'll go with you," Raina told her.

"You will?" Berry asked. "I thought you were angry at me."

Raina closed her book and slipped it back into her backpack. "I can see you are very sorry," she said. "And I don't want you to go by yourself. It's always better to fly with a friend."

Feeling overwhelmed, Berry reached out to hug her friend. "You are a good friend, Raina. Thank you."

"Melli and I will stay with Dash," Cocoa said. "I have some chocolate dots here that should keep her happy for a while."

"Thanks," Dash said. "But I don't really feel like eating right now."

Hearing Dash refuse candy made Berry move a little faster. Dash never declined a piece of candy!

"We'll go now," Berry told her. "We'll be back before bedtime. I promise you won't go to sleep a yellow Mint Fairy." She gave Dash a big hug and then waved to Melli and Cocoa. She was glad they'd be with Dash to look after her.

Together, Berry and Raina flew off toward Fruit Chew Meadow to gather orange blossoms for Lemona. Berry hoped with all her heart that the meeting would go well—and that Lemona could help get Dash back to normal. Otherwise, Heart Day was not going to be a happy day.

CHAPTER 6

Spooky Meadow

When Berry and Raina arrived at Fruit Chew Meadow, the sun had just slid to the other side of the Frosted Mountains. Berry flew over to the row of orange trees along the side of the meadow. The sweet citrus scent smelled delicious. Being in the meadow made Berry feel safe and relaxed. But she didn't have time to rest! If they wanted to talk to Lemona before the evening stars came out, she and Raina would have to hurry.

"How can anyone be mean *and* like orange blossoms?" Berry asked Raina. She put her nose close to the beautiful orange flower.

"Mmmm," Raina said. She flew over to Berry and smelled the flower candy. "I know what you mean. Sure as sugar, these do smell sweet." She thought for a moment and then looked up at Berry. "Maybe Sour Orchard Fairies aren't as sour as their candy. You know in the Fairy Code Book there is no mention of what the Sour Orchard Fairies are like—just the kind of candy they grow."

Berry raised her eyebrows. "Have you ever met a Sour Orchard Fairy?" she asked Raina.

 154

"No," Raina said slowly. "I've only seen one once, at Candy Castle last year at Candy Fair. She had green wings and a light green dress. I think she brought sour apple suckers to the castle."

Berry nodded. She remembered the fair last year, when all the fairies in the valley came to the summer celebration in the Royal Gardens. There were a few Sour Orchard Fairies there, but Berry hadn't talked to them. "They always look so . . ." She searched for the right word.

"Sour?" Raina asked, giggling. "I guess we don't really know, if we've never spoken to them." She helped Berry pick a few more blossoms from the tree. "Maybe we'll find out that Lemona is really a sweet fairy."

Berry put a bunch of the fragrant blossoms

in her basket. "Or maybe the Fairy Code Book suggests taking the blossoms to make sure the fairies don't get sour when a visitor comes." Her wings shook as she imagined having to face a sour fairy.

"Oh, Berry, your dress!" Raina cried.

Looking down, Berry saw orange stains on her new dress. "Oh, it's just as well," she said. "This dress wasn't really working for me anyway."

"Wait, did you just hear something rustling over there?" Raina asked, pointing to the ground. She squinted in the dark. "I don't like being here after Sun Dip."

"That must have been the wind," Berry told her. She flew down to the ground and looked around the trunk of the tree. "No one's here."

"Then where is that light coming from?" Raina asked, quivering. There was an eerie green glow getting closer and closer to the orange tree.

Berry turned around. Out of the darkness a fairy appeared.

"Aaaaah!" Berry and Raina screamed.

"Sorry," Fruli answered. "I didn't mean to scare you." She pointed her glowing peppermint candy at the ground. "I didn't think anyone would be here now," she said very softly.

Raina gasped. "Oh, Fruli!" she exclaimed. "You scared the sugar out of me!" Her hand flew to her chest. Her heart was beating so fast she could hardly breathe. "What arc you doing here?"

Fruli's wings began to beat even faster. "I . . . I . . . I like to come here when the day is over and smell the orange blossoms. The sweet smell

helps me to sleep. There are orange trees like this on Meringue Island, and the smell reminds me of home."

Berry was trying to get Raina's attention. She didn't want her mentioning to Fruli what they were doing. All Berry needed was for Fruli to know that she had picked sour wild cherry hearts—and given them to one of her best friends. Worse yet, she couldn't let her know that Dash was yellow because of her!

"We have to get going," Berry said quickly. She grabbed a shawl from her bag and covered her stained dress. Then she pulled on Raina's hand and took her to the other side of the meadow.

"Berry!" Raina cried. "We didn't even say good-bye. Why are you acting so rude?"

"Did you forget about Dash? She's yellow!

159

I'm just trying to get to Lemona as soon as possible," Berry explained.

"Fruli seems so nice," Raina said, shaking her head. "You could have at least asked her what she did for Sun Dip. Maybe she'd want to hang out with us. She seemed homesick."

"She's too fancy. She wouldn't want to hang out with us," Berry said. "Did you see her dress?" She sighed wistfully. "She has the most glamorous clothes. She'd never want to have Sun Dip with us. She'd want to be up at the castle or with the older Fruit Fairies."

Raina eyed her friend. "Maybe, but maybe not. Have you ever asked her?"

"Why are you on her side?" Berry snapped.

"I'm not," Raina said. "I just think you could have been a little sweeter to Fruli."

Berry huffed and rolled her eyes. "Raina, she's not some lost gummy cub." She packed up the orange blossoms and looked up at Raina. "What? I'm just saying that she's fine and we're late. Come on!"

Raina shook her head. When Berry had a mission, she was focused. She knew her Fruit Fairy friend could be stubborn. She was all juiced up. "Let's get going," Raina said. "I think we have enough orange blossoms for Lemona now."

Taking flight, Berry soared through the air. She had never ventured past Chocolate River to Sour Orchard. Being there at night made things seem even spookier. She hoped with all her heart that Lemona would tell them how they could help Dash. As Berry glided over the valley with

Raina, she held tightly to her basket of orange blossoms. If the sweet smell didn't sway the sour fairy, she hoped she and Raina could. She just had to have the answer that would help Dash. Berry's heart was breaking just thinking about Dash's being yellow. This plan had to work!

7

Brave Hearts

Sour Orchard was bursting with lemon, lime, cherry, apple, and orange trees. But these trees were different from the ones Berry and Raina were used to seeing in Fruit Chew Meadow and Gummy Forest. These trees grew in the tangy sugar crystals of Sour Orchard. Thick tree

trunks held up heavy branches filled with sweet and sour fruits.

Berry peered down at the orchard. "I wish it wasn't so dark," she said.

"I know," Raina said. "It's a little spooky here. But at least there's some moonlight."

"Let's fly lower so we can see better," Berry called. The orchard was much larger than Berry thought it would be. Even in the dim light, she could see that there were several rows of trees.

As she flew Berry looked at all the fruits on the trees. The thought of eating those sour candies made her mouth water. There were trees dripping with bunches of sour candy suckers and fruits.

Berry knew Fruit Chew Meadow so well that even in the dark she could find her way, but this place was different. The trees looked different and the smells were not the same.

"Thanks for coming with me," Berry whispered to Raina. She grabbed her hand. "I'm sorry I snapped at you before."

"It's okay," Raina said. "Besides, I wouldn't have let you come alone."

"You are a good friend," Berry told her. She squeezed her friend's hand tighter.

Berry spotted a familiar vine growing on a tree deep in the orchard. She pulled Raina along as she swooped down to look.

"Raina!" she exclaimed. "This is the same vine that was growing by Chocolate River! This is the magic heart vine!"

Berry landed next to the vine, and Raina followed. "Sure as sugar!" she said. "I knew those candies were magic hearts." She looked around. "Lemona must live somewhere around here."

Taking a walk around a lemon tree, Berry searched for a sign of the Sour Fairy. Her red boots crunched on the sour sugar coating the ground. "What does the Fairy Code Book say? What type of home does she have?"

"Look!" Raina exclaimed. She pointed to a sign on a lemon tree a few feet away. A small piece of fruit leather had "Lemona" etched on it. "She must live over there."

Lemona's house! Berry's heart began to race. She wasn't sure what to say to the fairy, but she knew she had to talk to her. She had to confess that she had given the candy to her friend without testing it first. As hard as that would be, Berry knew she had to find out the truth about the candy. And the secret of the magic hearts.

Before they stepped closer to the tree, a small sugar fly flew up to Berry. The messenger buzzed around her ears.

"You have a message for me?" Berry asked.

The sugar fly nodded and handed her the note. Immediately, Berry saw that the note was from Melli. Her breath caught in her chest and she gasped. "Oh, Raina! What if something horrible has happened?" she cried. Berry's wings started to flutter and she flew up in the air. "I will never forgive myself if something has happened to Dash. What was I thinking, giving out candy that I didn't know about!"

Raina touched Berry's arm. "Let's see what

the note says. We don't know what this is about yet."

Berry's hand was shaking. "I can't," she said, handing the note to Raina. "Would you please read this for me? I can't bear to read any more sour news today."

"Maybe the news isn't bad," Raina said. She tried to smile encouragingly at her friend.

"Please read it," Berry pleaded.

Raina opened the letter. "Dash is fine," she read. "But she is now orange! Please hurry and send along any information that you get." Raina looked up from the note. "Oh, sugar," she said. "This is worse than I thought."

Berry's eyes grew wide. "What do you mean?" she gasped.

"Well, she's turning more than one color,"

Raina said. "That's not a good sign."

Berry turned to see the sugar fly. He was waiting for a return note. Quickly, Berry scribbled a message back to her friends. "We'll soon be on our way with help," she said as she wrote the note. "Hold on. We've just arrived at the orchard." She folded up the note and handed it to the sugar fly. "Please give this to Melli or Cocoa," she instructed the sugar fly.

"Are you all right?" Raina asked, looking at Berry.

Suddenly Berry was juiced up. Dash needed her help, and she was going to get her out of this sour mess. She wasn't going to be afraid. She was simply going to ask Lemona what was in her candy and how to help get Dash back to normal.

 170

"Let's not dip our wings in syrup yet!" Berry said. She put her hands on her hips, charged with confidence. "We're here, aren't we? We need to have brave hearts!"

Raina grinned. Her spunky friend was back! And just in time. If they were going to talk to Lemona, they needed to be brave and confident.

"Lemona will help us," Berry said. With a burst of hope, she walked toward Lemona's tree.

Just then a cloud passed over the full moon, blocking the bright moonlight for a brief moment. Berry and Raina stood still in the middle of Sour Orchard, unsure of what to do. They were so close to Lemona's tree, but they couldn't see a thing!

CHAPTER

8

Sweet Sours

L icking lollipops!" Berry cried. "It's too dark!" How could they talk to Lemona if they couldn't find her front door?

"Wait," Raina said. "I have those peppermint candies that Dash gave us before we left." She dug around into her bag and pulled out a bright candy.

Berry smiled. "When we get back, we'll have to thank Dash for giving those to us," she said.

In the pale green light of the glowing peppermint, the two fairies were able to find their way to Lemona's tree.

Berry paused before knocking on the door. There was a strong scent of lemon in the air, and Berry turned to Raina. "Ready?" she asked.

"If you are," the Gummy Fairy said, trying to sound brave.

Berry took a deep breath and knocked on the door. The door opened, and there stood a small, older fairy.

"Hello," the fairy said. She peered over her glasses to look at Berry and Raina. "Two young fairies at my door past Sun Dip?" she asked. "What brings you two here?"

"We've come for some help," Berry said bravely.

The older fairy nodded, and opened her door wider to invite them in. Her pale yellow hair was pulled back in a tight bun, and her wings and her dress were both yellow. "Come in," she said kindly.

Berry and Raina walked into the fairy's house. Berry eyed Lemona. Her yellow dress was simple and neat, and her wings were gold. She had large almond-shaped eyes that were a bright green, complementing her blond hair. She didn't look sour and mean, but Berry couldn't be so sure.

Lemona strode over to a chair near the fireplace. There was a large yellow cauldron on the fire and a plate of lemon drop candies

on a table. She stirred the pot and dropped a few lemon candies in. A poof of smoke flew from the pot. Lemona sat down in her chair and waved to Berry and Raina to have a seat on a small couch.

"What are you cooking?" Raina asked. She smelled the air. "Whatever it is, it smells delicious."

"It's a lemon broth for the candy hearts I am making," she said. She settled herself in her chair. "I'm getting too old for this!" she exclaimed as she leaned back into the chair. "Heart Day always sneaks up on me and I wind up rushing."

Berry nodded. She knew exactly how Lemona felt!

"Actually, that is why we're here," Berry said. She took a deep breath and told Lemona her story. As she sat by the fire she was amazed how easy it was to talk to Lemona. Berry wound up telling her all about Fruli and how she wanted to make a new dress. Then she explained how she had found the magic hearts.

"All the way by Chocolate River?" Lemona remarked. "My sweet sours, I have never heard of the wind carrying the seeds that far!"

"You mean this has happened before?" Raina asked. She sat on the edge of her seat, listening. This should be entered in the Fairy Code Book!

The older fairy nodded. "Yes, sometimes the strong winter winds make the seeds take flight." She reached over to stir the pot. "What did you do with the candy?"

Berry looked down at her hands in her lap. "Well, I let my friend Dash the Mint Fairy eat one," Berry told Lemona. "I know that I shouldn't have done that." She looked up at Lemona. "Now Dash is turning colors. She was yellow and now she's orange!"

Lemona shook her head. "I'm sorry to hear that," she said. "You know that candy doesn't always look the way it tastes."

"Yes, ma'am," Berry said. She kept her eyes on the ground. She was more embarrassed than ever. That is one of the first rules of candy making.

Lemona heaved herself out of her chair and walked over to the pantry. She opened up the cupboard and took out a jar. Inside were brightly colored crystal sugars, and Lemona poured a stream into the pot. "And how is Dash feeling?" she asked.

"She seems to be fine," Berry told her. "Except

her color is off. She doesn't want to be a yellow or orange Mint Fairy."

"I understand," Lemona said.

Berry couldn't believe how kind Lemona was being. When she sat and talked to the young fairies, she didn't have a sour face at all! In fact, Lemona was being so sweet that Berry started to relax.

"Those wild flavors are a bit tricky at times," Lemona finally said. She stood up to add a few more lemon drops in the cauldron.

"Can you help Dash?" Berry asked.

"I believe I know just the thing for your Mint Fairy friend," Lemona said thoughtfully. She pulled a book down from the shelf behind her.

Raina's eyes widened. She had never seen

 179

that book before. She leaned over to get a closer look at *Sour Orchard, Volume III.*

"Will it say in there what to do?" Berry asked anxiously.

Lemona wrapped a yellow shawl around her arms carefully. "Let me just make sure," she said.

Berry glanced over at Raina. She hoped this trip to Sour Orchard would turn out to be worth their while. She couldn't bear to get another sugar fly message that Dash had turned yet another color!

Please, please, Berry wished as Lemona bent over the large book, *please find what you are looking for in there!*

 181

CHAPTER
9

A Peppermint Plan

Berry and Raina sat on the edge of their seats as Lemona reviewed the large Sour Orchard history book. The two fairies watched as Lemona slowly turned the pages. She stopped once to take a sip from her yellow teacup. It was so hard to wait patiently as Lemona tried to find the answer to their question. This was worse than waiting for fruit-chew jewelry to dry!

Looking around the room, Berry noticed that Lemona had many pieces of art hanging in her home. Lemona reminded Berry of her great-aunt Razz. She was a wise and beloved Fruit Fairy. Razz had pieces of art hanging in her home too. Berry never would have imagined that she would feel so comfortable in a Sour Orchard Fairy's house! She couldn't wait to get back and tell Cocoa, Melli, and Dash. That is, if Lemona could solve Dash's dilemma.

Raina looked over at Berry and smiled.

Berry was so glad her good friend was with her. "I wouldn't have been able to do this without you," she whispered.

"Oh, sure you would have," Raina said,

swatting her hand. "But I am happy to be here now. And I think Lemona is going to be able to help us."

At that moment Lemona spoke up. "Oh, here it is!" she exclaimed. She took off her lemon-colored glasses and waved them in the air. "I knew it was in here somewhere."

"Oh, please tell us," Berry pleaded. "I want Dash to be back to her normal mint self."

"It's just as I had thought," Lemona said. She peered over at Berry. "This will take some work, and you'll have to act quickly."

"Anything for Dash!" Berry declared.

"Tell us what we need to do," Raina said.

Pointing to the open page, Lemona read the instructions. "You must gather leaves from Peppermint Grove," she said. "The leaves must be fresh from the vine, not from the ground." She gazed up at the two fairies.

Both Berry and Raina nodded.

"Fresh mint leaves," Berry repeated.

Lemona returned her attention to the book and continued to read. "Make a strong cup of peppermint tea," she instructed. "Eat three peppermint candies from the old mint tree in the northern part of Peppermint Grove, and get plenty of rest." Lemona looked up at the two young fairies. "If she does all that, in the morning she'll wake up her own self."

Berry popped off her seat. "Peppermint tea will cure her?" she asked.

Lemona nodded.

185

"You'd be surprised how many ailments are cured by peppermint tea!"

Raina stood up. "I know the tree you are talking about," she said. "We'll get those things to Dash straightaway."

"Thank you very much," Berry said to Lemona. "You have been so helpful." Then she paused for a moment. "Thank you for being so sweet to us."

The Sour Orchard Fairy threw her head back and laughed. "Oh, please," she said. "We all make mistakes. I hope you've learned that you can't assume a candy is a certain way because of its color and shape."

"Yes!" Berry exclaimed.

Sure as sugar, she thought. She would never again assume any candy would be a certain way.

 186

She pulled off two candy jewels from her dress and handed them to Lemona. "I'd like to give you something."

"Did you make these?" Lemona asked. "They are beautiful."

"Thank you," Berry said, blushing. "I'd love for you to have them. They make neat hair clips," she added.

Lemona reached out and gave Berry a hug. And Berry gave the yellow fairy a tight squeeze back.

"We must get going," Berry said. "We've got to get Dash her tea."

"Yes, it's getting late," Raina added. "We should be going."

Lemona stood up and walked the fairies to the door. "Thank you for coming," she said. "And for the candy jewels."

"Thank you," Raina said. "It really was a pleasure to meet you. Will we see you at Heart Day?"

Lemona smiled. "Of course," she said. "I love Heart Day. I'll be there, and I'd love to see you and your Mint Fairy friend as well."

"Licking lollipops!" Berry said. "We all wouldn't miss it for the world."

For the first time since Dash had taken a bite of the magic heart candy, Berry had hope that everything could go back to normal. She may not have a new dress to wear to Heart Day, but maybe Dash would be back to herself for the celebration.

As fast as fairies can fly, Berry and Raina flew to Peppermint Grove and got the peppermint leaves for the tea and the three candies. Then they quickly flew to Red Licorice Lake, where they knew Melli, Cocoa, and Dash were waiting.

"They're back!" Cocoa cried when she spotted her friends in the air. "Did you find Lemona?"

"Was she sour like Mogu?" Melli asked. "Or did she agree to help you?"

Berry looked around. There were a few peppermints giving off a soft glow to light up the area. "Where's Dash?"

"I'm here," Dash said. Her voice was muffled.

"Where are you, Dash?" Berry asked. She looked to Melli and Cocoa. Both of her friends pointed to a stack of picked licorice stalks.

"She hasn't come out of there since she started to turn orange," Cocoa told her.

Berry knelt down and peered inside the nest of licorice. "Dash, can you come out? It's just us. Raina and I have something for you."

"Will it make me return to my normal color?" Dash asked. "I'm red now!"

Melli's hand flew to her mouth. "Hot caramel," she said. "This is getting serious."

"Don't worry," Berry said. "We found Lemona, and you just need to drink some peppermint tea and eat some peppermint candy."

"All things you love," Raina added. "And we picked everything fresh from the grove. Honest." She peered over Berry's shoulder to look into the licorice nest. "Fairy Code honor."

There was a bit of rustling, and a few licorice stalks shifted. Dash's head popped out. "No laughing!" she said, her hands covering her face.

"Oh, Dash," Berry said. "I don't care what color you are, you will always be my friend."

"But look at me!" Dash cried. "I'm red!"

Raina stepped forward. "But not for long, Dash." She handed her a candy teacup of peppermint tea, and the three peppermint candies. "Lemona said to have these and then get a good night's rest."

Dash took the tea and candy from Raina and gulped everything down. She sat down on the red sugar sand and peered up at her friends.

"Do I look any different?" she asked.

"Not yet," Berry said.

"You match the sand," Cocoa blurted out.

Melli shot Cocoa a stern look.

"But I'm sure you'll be feeling like yourself soon," Cocoa added quickly.

"Lemona was so sweet, Dash," Berry told her. "She looked up the problem in a book and was so willing to help. In the morning you'll be feeling minty fresh, sure as sugar!"

Dash pulled the hood of her sweater over her head. "I hope you're right," she said. "Otherwise, there is no way I'm going to Heart Day like this."

Berry's heart sank. Heart Day without Dash? That would be awful! This peppermint plan had to work.

CHAPTER 10

True Hearts

Berry raced across Sugar Valley in the early morning light. She was rushing to get to Dash's house. She hoped that when Dash greeted her at the door, her friend would look like herself. She couldn't bear to see Dash red, pink, purple, or any other color!

The Royal Gardens were already set up for

the Heart Day celebration. From the sky above, Berry could see that the Castle Fairies were hard at work. There were small red and pink candy hearts draped from the tall sugar gates, and large heart-shaped candies hung from the royal candy trees. It was one gigantic heart fest!

Sighing, Berry hoped the day would go as she had planned. She wanted to be at the party with *all* her friends. She knew that if Dash wasn't herself, the proud Mint Fairy would not go to the castle party. And that would be all Berry's fault!

Berry raced up to Dash's door. She knocked several times. Berry was not known for her patience, and the Fruit Fairy couldn't wait a second longer at Dash's doorstep.

"I'm coming!" Dash finally cried from the

other side. As she opened the door, the bright morning light made her squint. She rubbed her eyes. "Berry?" she said. "What are you doing here so early?"

"I wanted to come see you first thing!" she blurted out. For the first time ever Berry was extremely early! She had jumped out of bed and quickly dressed. She wanted to be at Dash's side when she woke up.

"Holy peppermint," Dash said. "I don't think I've ever seen you anywhere so early!"

Berry didn't even respond. She pulled Dash out into the bright sunlight. She gasped and reached out to give Dash a hug. "You look like your old minty self!" she cried.

"Never underestimate the power of peppermint tea," Dash said, grinning. "I am feeling

 196

much better." She smiled up at Berry. "And looking much better too," she added. She rolled up her sleeves and grinned at her normal color. She was back!

"Oh, Dash," Berry gushed. "I am so glad! Sweet strawberries! This is going to be a great day!"

"But you didn't have a chance to make your heart candy or finish your new outfit," Dash said. She eyed Berry's dress. "And you're not even wearing the new dress you made."

"Don't make that sour face," Berry said, smiling. "That other dress was stained. Besides, I love this red dress. It's red for Heart Day!" She twirled around in front of Dash. "Look, I even added a sugar crystal heart here on the waistband." Berry leaned down and showed

Dash the sparkly heart she had sewn on. "I'm going to give Princess Lolli my heart-shaped fruit-chew barrettes."

"Princess Lolli will love those. And you always look fantastic," Dash said. "Even when you are rushed!" She turned back and called over her shoulder. "I'll be ready in a minty minute!"

Just as Dash ducked back behind her door, Melli, Raina, and Cocoa flew up. Each of them held their heart candies for Heart Day. Before they could say anything, Berry blurted out the good news about Dash.

"Dash is looking *so mint*!" Berry shouted. "It's truly a happy Heart Day after all."

"A day of hearts and true friendship," Raina cheered.

Berry nodded. "Thank you," she said.

"I've really learned my lesson. And I've been thinking . . ."

"Oh no," Cocoa said. "What are you up to now, Berry?"

Laughing, Berry walked over to Cocoa and gave her hand a squeeze. "I was just thinking that I haven't been very sweet to a new Fruit Fairy."

"You mean Fruli?" Raina asked.

"Who's Fruli?" Melli said.

Berry hung her head. "Fruli is from Meringue Island. She's new to Sugar Valley. Instead of trying to be nice to her, I've just been very jealous of her. And that's the ugliest and most sour way to be," she admitted.

"Is she going to be at Heart Day?" Melli asked.

"I hope so," Berry said. "I'd like you all to meet her."

Raina smiled at Berry. "You were thinking about what Lemona told you, huh?"

"Yes," Berry confessed. "I was thinking the same thing could be true about fairies, not just candies. I never took the time to get to know Fruli. Maybe she's different from what I thought."

"A perfect plan for Heart Day," Melli said.

"Yes, and the real meaning of Heart Day," Raina said.

"It's not just a party. It's a celebration of good friends," Cocoa chimed in.

"You can be sure as sugar it's a celebration!" Dash said as she zoomed out of her house. "Let's go have a heart feast!"

Together, the five fairies flew to the Royal

Gardens. There were already many fairies gathered in a line to see Princess Lolli. Lemona waved and winked at Berry when she saw her holding Dash's hand.

"Nice to see you all here," Lemona said as she flew by.

"Hello, Lemona!" Berry called out. She noticed that Lemona had put the candy jewels in her hair for the party.

"Was that a Sour Orchard Fairy?" Dash asked.

"Yes," Berry replied. "And one of the sweetest fairies you'll ever meet."

When the fairy friends joined the line to greet Princess Lolli, Berry spotted Fruli. She was dressed in a beautiful soft pink chiffon dress and was holding a cherry red heart-shaped box.

202

"Hi, Fruli," Berry called. "I'd like you to meet some of my friends." Berry introduced everyone and then smiled at Fruli. "And I want to apologize to you. I haven't been very nice. Please accept my apology."

A smile spread across Fruli's face. "Thank you," she said. She looked right at Berry as she spoke. "It's been hard being the new fairy. I would love to meet some new friends."

"And Heart Day is just the day for making new friends!" Princess Lolli said. She greeted the fairies and gave them each a hug. "Thank you all for coming and for these wonderful heart gifts." She looked over at Berry. "And I see you have found the true message of Heart Day already."

Berry beamed. "Sure as sugar!" she cried.

She looked around at her good friends, and her new friends. Meeting Lemona and Fruli had made this an extra-special Heart Day. No candy heart was sweeter than making new friends!

The
Sugar Ball

For Karli and Hana Grace Meyer

Sweet Thoughts

Cocoa smiled as she flew across Chocolate
Woods. The sun was shining and the air was full
of sweet, rich chocolate scents. The Chocolate
Fairy spread her golden wings and glided down
to Chocolate Falls. *Yum*, thought Cocoa as she
licked her lips. There was nothing better than
fresh milk chocolate.

"Cocoa!" Melli the Caramel Fairy called. "Over here!" Melli was sitting underneath a chocolate oak tree. She waved to get Cocoa's attention.

Waving back, Cocoa fluttered down to her friend's side. Melli was always on time—or early. She was a shy fairy, but her sweet caramel nature was part of what kept their group of friends sticking together—no matter what.

"What a *choc-o-rific* day!" Cocoa sang. She smiled at her friend.

"Only one more week until the Sugar Ball," Melli burst out. "I can't wait!" She took out a light caramel twist from her bag. "What do you think? I just had to show you right away." She held up the long caramel rope candy for Cocoa to view.

"It looks delicious," Cocoa commented.

"Won't this be perfect for the sash on my dress?" Melli asked. "I've been searching for just the right size trim."

Cocoa laughed. All any of her friends could think about was the Sugar Ball at Candy Castle and the dresses they'd wear to the party. The big ball was the grandest—and sweetest—of the season. The Sugar Ball was a celebration of the sugar harvest. Fairies from all over came to the Royal Gardens for the party. Princess Lolli, the ruling fairy princess, always made the party the most scrumptious of the year.

"I think that will be the perfect addition to your outfit," Cocoa said. She touched the golden caramel twist. "This is the exact right color for your dress."

 213

Melli clapped her hands. "I knew you'd say that!" she said, grinning. "Cara wanted me to make her one just like this too."

Cara was Melli's little sister and always wanted to be just like her big sister.

"Did you help her?" Cocoa asked.

"Sure as sugar," Melli said. "She's so excited about her first ball." She stopped and admired her dress. "Now I just need to find the right necklace."

"You should ask Berry to make you one of her sparkly fruit-chew necklaces," Cocoa said. She was used to her friend Berry the Fruit Fairy always talking about fashion, but this year all her friends were concerned about their Sugar Ball dresses and jewelry. Everyone wanted to make her ball gown special and unique. Even Cocoa!

"You're right," Melli said. "I should ask Berry. I just hope she doesn't say she's too busy. Did you know that she is weaving the material for her dress herself? Her dress is going to be *sweet-tacular*!"

"Hmm," Cocoa muttered. She was actually growing a little tired of all the talk about dresses. Even though she wanted to look her best, she had another idea of how to make her entrance at the ball special.

"Do you think Char will remember me?" Melli asked, interrupting Cocoa's thoughts. Her light brown eyes had a faraway gaze. Like most fairies in Sugar Valley, she loved the Sugar Pops. They were brothers who played in a band together and sang the sweetest songs. Char was the lead singer in the band and Melli's supersweet crush.

"How could they forget you?" Cocoa asked. "You were the Candy Fairy who saved Caramel Moon!" In the fall, when the candy corn crop was in danger, Melli was the one who discovered the problem. Together with their fairy friends, they saved the Caramel Moon festival, where the Sugar Pops played. They even got to meet Carob, Chip, and Char! Seeing them again at the Sugar Ball would definitely sugarcoat the night.

"I know it's just a rumor that they'll come," Melli said, "but I hope the sugar fly buzz is right. I would love to see them again." Melli clasped her hands together and put them under her chin. She looked over at Cocoa. "What's in your bag?"

Looking down at her bag, Cocoa smiled. There were a couple of strands of marshmallow threads sticking out of her chocolate weave bag. "I was down at Marshmallow Marsh this morning," she explained.

"What are you doing with marshmallow?" Melli asked. "You can't use that for your dress. Marshmallow is too sticky to work for an outfit."

Cocoa laughed. "No, not for my dress," she said. "Something else for the ball." She sat down and took out a sheet of paper from her pocket. "Last week when Raina was reading from the Fairy Code Book, there was that story about the princess and her chocolate scepter. Do you remember?"

Raina the Gummy Fairy was their good friend, who loved to read. She had nearly memorized the entire Fairy Code Book!

Nodding, Melli thought back to the story. "It was a magic scepter made of the finest sugar. The picture in the book showed a beautiful chocolate wand."

"Yes," Cocoa said, "and I was thinking that I'd like to make a chocolate scepter for the ball. Wouldn't that be so sweet, to walk in holding a royal scepter?" Cocoa sighed. "I'd be like a fairy princess!"

Just thinking about the scepter made Cocoa's wings flutter. Even though she was excited about her new strawberry-and-chocolate dot dress with a purple candy butterfly, she couldn't wait to hold a royal scepter. "It will be like a magic wand!"

"You will look like a fairy princess," Melli agreed. Then she paused. "Do you know how to make a magic wand?"

Cocoa shook her head. "No, but I plan on learning. I made a sketch of the scepter that I'd like to make." She held up her drawing. "Did you bring me the caramel ball mold? I wanted

to have a round chocolate sphere at the top."

Melli pulled the round mold out of her bag and gave it to Cocoa. "I was wondering what you were going to do with this," she said.

"I'm meeting Raina later," Cocoa told her. "She's going to lend me a book about magic wands." Carefully, Cocoa folded her drawing up and put the paper back in her bag. "I thought the marshmallow would add a nice touch."

"I think you're right." Melli nodded.

"And I'll need lots of this chocolate," Cocoa added. She took out a pail and dipped it into the pool of chocolate swirling in front of her. "The waterfall chocolate is the best for making special chocolate candies. I need to hurry home so the chocolate can set. Then I'm going to carve decorations on the ball."

"I can't wait to see that chocolate wand!" Melli cried.

"Thanks," Cocoa replied. She swept up her bucket and headed back to Chocolate Woods. She had lots of work to do before Sun Dip tonight. A chocolate magic wand was no small task. And Cocoa wanted to make sure it was going to be the talk of the Sugar Ball.

CHAPTER

2

The Chocolate Scepter

When Cocoa returned to Chocolate Woods, she poured the fresh chocolate into Melli's hard caramel mold. She knew that she wanted a chocolate ball at the top of her wand—just like the one she had seen in Raina's book. Later, when the chocolate was hard, she would carefully carve the ball with her tools. Oh, she couldn't wait! Her magic scepter was going to be *choc-o-rific*!

While the chocolate was hardening, Cocoa flew to Gummy Forest to find Raina. Her friend had not one, as promised, but two books on magic wands.

"You should know that it's often sticky business to make magic wands," Raina told her. She pushed her long hair out of her eyes as she spoke. "If wands get into the wrong hands, there can be trouble."

Cocoa laughed. "Oh, chocolate sticks," she said. "It's just for my costume. Raina, you worry too much. And I don't think I am going to let go of it. I've been working so hard on the wand. I'll want to hold my perfect accessory all evening!"

Raina handed the two large books to Cocoa.

"Here you go," she said. "These are two books that have a few different pictures of royal scepters."

Flipping through the pages, Cocoa's eyes grew wide with excitement. "Oh, this is perfect!" she exclaimed. She noticed the details in the chocolate carvings and the bright colors used for the wands. She had so many ideas, and she wanted to get started right away.

Cocoa felt a gentle nudge and looked down. "Hi, Nokie," she said. Nokie was a little red gummy bear cub. He was always hungry. Even though he didn't eat chocolate, he was hoping that Cocoa might have a treat for him. "I have some fruit chews, if you want," she told him. "Berry gave them to me yesterday, and I'm not going to use them for my hair clips."

Nokie eagerly nodded. Berry had given him fruit chews before and he loved the fruity, sparkly candy.

"Nokie!" Raina scolded. But she couldn't help smiling at the cute cub when she saw his face. Her voice softened. "Just one, okay?"

The gummy cub quickly agreed and took Cocoa's offering.

"Sorry about that," Raina apologized to Cocoa. "No matter how much I feed Nokie, he's always hungry!"

Cocoa patted the friendly cub on his belly. "It's okay," she said. "I'm happy to share."

"Do you want to see my dress?" Raina asked. "The color came out perfectly!" She showed her friend the bright lime-green dress with rainbow gummy accents on the waist and hem. She held the gown up to show off the details.

"Oh, Raina," Cocoa gasped. "This is really beautiful. You made this by yourself?"

Raina blushed. "Well, I had some help from Berry. She's so good at designing and sewing. I'm not sure what I would have done without her."

"You are going to look delicious," Cocoa told her. "Have you decided how you'll wear your hair?"

Raina shrugged. "I'm not sure yet," she confided. "Maybe I'll get a fancy updo. What do you think?" She pulled her long, straight hair up and twisted it in a fancy bun. "I could use a rainbow gummy berry for a clip."

"I can't wait to see what you decide," Cocoa told her. "Sure as sugar, every fairy in Sugar

Valley is going to look extra-sweet."

"I know!" Raina exclaimed. "I can't wait!"

Cocoa glanced over at the Frosted Mountains. "I better get going," she said. "I want to carve the chocolate ball before Sun Dip tonight." She winked at Raina. "Maybe I'll bring the wand for a special preview."

"Oh, please do!" Raina pleaded. "I'd love to see what you do." She took Nokie's paw and gave a wave to her friend. "I've got to take Nokie back to his den. I'll see you later."

"Thanks for the books," Cocoa called. She took off and flew swiftly back to Chocolate Woods.

At home Cocoa saw the chocolate in her mold was hard and dry. She selected the smallest pink sugar crystal carving tool for the delicate design of the chocolate wand. The tiny tool was good for small details. She glanced over at one of the books Raina had given her. She was looking at a couple of different wands and using ideas that she loved about each one. Skillfully she carved a beautiful design on the chocolate ball.

When she finished she stood back and gazed at her sphere. She placed the ball on top of the wand using very hot chocolate and sugar. Then she added a few glittering candy jewels that she had been saving for a special occasion and a bit of white marshmallow as a finishing touch.

She pointed the wand at a cracker on the table, and instantly it was covered in chocolate.

"Hot chocolate!" she exclaimed. "I really did it!"

The lavender light seeping through her window alerted her to the time. Her friends were probably already gathered for Sun Dip. She took her wand, eager for her friends to see her handiwork.

As she had suspected all her friends were together near the shores of Red Licorice Lake for Sun Dip. Even Berry was there! Berry was hardly ever on time, but she must have been very excited to show off her new fruit-chew jewelry and her ball gown.

"Did you finish your wand?" Melli called out as soon as she spotted Cocoa.

Cocoa proudly took her prized possession out of her bag. She floated above her friends and waved her royal scepter. Tiny little pieces of chocolate sprinkled from the wand, and her friends giggled as they grabbed for the sweets.

"So mint!" Dash called out. The little Mint Fairy was the smallest fairy in Sugar Valley, but also one of the fastest. She swooped through the air to gather up the most chocolate. "Cocoa, your wand is beautiful—and *choc-o-rific!*"

"You certainly have a way with chocolate," Melli said.

"Thanks," Cocoa said, grinning. "I can't wait for the ball. We're going to have the best time!"

"And wait till the Sugar Pops see us!" Melli gushed.

"They won't even recognize us," Berry boasted. "The last time we saw them, we weren't in ball gowns. We'd been working in Candy Corn Fields!" She slipped her long gown on over her dress. "Cocoa, will you zip me up?"

 231

"Sure," Cocoa said, setting down the wand. "This gown is *sweet-tacular*!"

Berry twirled around in a circle. The meringue bottom of her dress fell around her in a puffed-out skirt. "I feel like a princess!" she said, beaming.

"And you look like one too," Raina told her. "I think we all will tomorrow night!"

"I better get back home," Cocoa said. She looked up at the sky. The sun was almost behind the Frosted Mountains. "I have to finish my dress." She grabbed her royal wand and put it in her bag. "I'll see you fairies tomorrow!" she cried as she shot up in the air. "I can't wait for the Sugar Ball!"

CHAPTER
3

Chocolate Clues

Speeding through Sugar Valley, Cocoa was grinning as she thought about the Sugar Ball. She wondered what Princess Lolli would say about her wand; after all, she was a *real* fairy princess. The ruling princess of Candy Kingdom certainly knew all about royal wands. Cocoa had long admired the fancy bejeweled candy scepter that Princess Lolli held at important affairs. Her great-grandmother Queen Taffy had passed down the wand to her. It was beautiful and sparkled with the most exquisite rainbow sugar candies. Cocoa hoped Princess Lolli would be pleased with her chocolate one!

When she arrived home, she put her bag on the chocolate oak table and examined her unfinished dress. She wanted to put a few extra chocolate sprinkles on the waistband.

As she sewed, Cocoa thought about the ball. Sugar Ball was known for elaborate candies made specially by the Royal Fairies at Candy Castle. Everything at the ball was sugarcoated and delicious! Holding a wand all night might be difficult. If she were to eat any candy, she'd need a free hand. Maybe if she sewed a loop on the side of the dress, she could easily slip the wand in and out.

Cocoa was very pleased with herself. What a *choc-o-rific* idea! She cut some extra fabric and got to work.

The stars twinkled in the dark night sky, and the full moon cast a white glow through Cocoa's window. She'd been hard at work for hours! Cocoa stood back and examined her finished gown. She was so proud of her dress—and the fancy loop on the side of the dress for the wand. Grabbing her chocolate weave bag from the table, she reached inside for her wand to test out her invention.

"Huh?" Cocoa murmured to herself. She stuck her hand into her bag. Where was the wand?

She knew she had put the wand back into her bag before leaving Sun Dip. She never would have left the wand lying on the ground. . . .

She searched the bag again. And then she saw her finger poking through a hole at the bottom of her bag. A hole that was big enough for her chocolate wand to fall through!

"Bittersweet chocolate!" she cried.

Cocoa's heart began to race. Her magic wand was gone? Raina's words rang in Cocoa's head. *If wands get into the wrong hands, there can be trouble.*

The first sour thought that came into Cocoa's head was of the salty old troll Mogu. Mogu lived under the bridge in Black Licorice Swamp and was always on the hunt for Candy Fairy candy. He had even stolen Cocoa's prized chocolate eggs from their nest in Chocolate

Woods. Cocoa's wings fluttered as she remembered her journey to Black Licorice Swamp with Princess Lolli. The princess had been brave as well as clever, and together, the two fairies had outsmarted that old troll. Would he have tried to steal from her again?

Cocoa rushed outside and called for the sugar flies. She had to get messages to her friends quickly. Sugar flies could be gossips, but they were also good for getting messages to friends in a hurry.

Dashing off notes to her friends, Cocoa instructed the flies to deliver the urgent messages. Cocoa knew it was late, but she asked her friends to meet her back at Red Licorice Lake. Since that was the last time she'd seen the wand, she figured she would begin her search there.

After the sugar flies took flight, Cocoa flew to the Sun Dip meeting spot. She hoped that on her way she'd spot the wand. Even though the moonlight was bright, Cocoa didn't see any candy jewels glittering on the ground. All that hard work—and all that chocolate magic! Cocoa was melting inside. How could she have been so careless? She should have double-checked her bag!

At Red Licorice Lake, Cocoa took a peppermint light from her pocket. She held the candy up as she searched the red sugar sand beach.

Not a trace of her wand.

Cocoa sat down on the cool red sugar sand. The valley was dark, and most fairies were home getting ready for bed. Her wings drooped as she thought about having to tell Princess

Lolli her wand had been lost. A magic wand gone missing was not something to take lightly. She'd have to tell her. If Mogu had gotten hold of the wand, there was no telling what would happen! The Sugar Ball would be canceled. All of Sugar Valley would be in danger. A troll with a magic wand . . . She didn't even want to think about it.

Cocoa pulled her knees up to her chest and buried her head. She hoped that the sugar flies had delivered her messages quickly and that her friends would come soon. Maybe together they'd be able to figure out what to do.

Glancing up, Cocoa saw a thick licorice stalk in front of her. She squinted in the moonlight, unsure of what she was looking at. What was on the top of the stalk? She stood up and flew to the top of the licorice.

It was covered in chocolate syrup!

Someone definitely found the wand here, Cocoa thought. The wand must have fallen out as soon as she took flight! Flying around the stalk, Cocoa wondered why someone would have aimed at the licorice stalk. She floated back down to the ground, searching for more clues. If she followed the chocolate clues, she'd find the wand!

She wasn't sure her plan would work, but she knew one thing. Sure as sugar, she needed all her friends to help her!

CHAPTER 4

Spreading Chocolate

Cocoa!" Melli cried. She swooped down and knelt near her friend. "Oh, Cocoa, what is going on?" She took a deep breath. "I saw chocolate puddles everywhere as I flew from Caramel Hills!"

Looking up at her friend, Cocoa's lip quivered. She didn't want to burst into tears, so she looked back down at her knees. "My wand . . . ," she began.

Melli's hand was on her back. "Oh, Cocoa. You worked so hard on that wand." And then she took a quick breath as she realized what this news meant. "And now someone has chocolate power!" she gasped.

"Licking lollipops!" Berry blurted out when she saw her friends. "What is going on here tonight? There's a chocolate explosion around here. You should see Fruit Chew Meadow! Those candy chews are going to need a power wash to get back to their fruity glory."

"There's chocolate in Fruit Chew Meadow, too?" Cocoa asked. She shook her head. This was worse than she had thought. Someone was definitely using the wand—someone who didn't understand the magic of chocolate.

"Strange," Berry said. She tapped her finger to her chin. "It's like there's a chocolate spell on Sugar Valley or something."

"And that spell is *so mint*!" Dash announced as she flew in from over the licorice stalks. "These peppermints are delicious with the chocolate sprayed on them. What a minty cool idea." She popped a chocolate-covered candy in her mouth and then licked her fingers.

"Dash!" Melli scolded. "This isn't a joke. Cocoa's magic wand has been stolen!"

"Not stolen, exactly," Cocoa said sadly. "My wand fell out of my bag when I left Sun Dip." She couldn't keep back her tears anymore. "And now this is all my fault! Raina warned me about making a magic wand."

Cocoa's friends all gasped. A gentle breeze blew and fluttered their wings as the fairies stood in silence.

"Oh, this doesn't look good," Raina said as she joined her friends. She looked at Cocoa. "I came as soon as I got the message. What happened?"

"Please tell me you know a story in the Fairy Code Book about a magic wand that gets into the wrong hands," Cocoa pleaded. She held up her bag and stuck her fingers in the hole. "My wand fell out after I left Sun Dip."

"Hot caramel," Melli muttered. "This is really a sticky situation." Then she realized why Cocoa was so upset. "Do you think Mogu could have picked up the wand?"

"Mogu can't make chocolate," Berry argued. "He's a troll."

"No, but if he is holding a magic wand that was made by a chocolate fairy," Raina said, thinking out loud, "then it might be possible."

Cocoa jumped up from the ground. "What do you mean, *might be possible?*" She grabbed Raina's hand. "You mean in all the stories you've ever read, you've never come across this?" She hung her head. "Oh, this is really bad."

Raina paced back and forth on the red sugar sand. "I don't know," she said. "I'm thinking."

The fairies all watched Raina. They weren't used to seeing her flustered. Raina was always so sure and logical. And usually she could quote a line from the Fairy Code Book that would solve their problem.

"But Raina always knows the answer!" Dash blurted out.

Berry and Melli shot her a look, but Dash just shrugged.

"Raina said it *might* be possible," Berry said. "Maybe there's hope that Mogu couldn't make this chocolate mess."

"That's a chance we can't take," Cocoa said. She stood up. "We need to follow the chocolate trail. Tracking the clues is the only way to find the wand."

Raina nodded. "Cocoa's right. Let's try to figure out where the wand is . . ."

"And who has it," Berry finished for her.

"What if Mogu did take the wand?" Melli asked. She shivered as she thought of the old troll having chocolate power. "What a gooey mess we're in! And right before the Sugar Ball."

"It's my mess," Cocoa said. "I'm going to fly

north toward Candy Castle. From your reports, the chocolate seems to be spreading in that direction."

"You are not going alone," Melli said, standing next to her.

"Sure as sugar, we're all going with you," Raina added.

Dash and Berry nodded. And they all leaned in to hug Cocoa.

"Thank you," Cocoa managed to say. "This means so much to me. I can't bear the thought of facing Princess Lolli with another chocolate mess."

"Don't get your wings stuck in syrup yet," Berry teased. "We can solve this mystery."

Together, the fairies flew to Candy Castle. The pink-and-white sugarcoated castle glistened in the moonlight. The frosted towers and iced tips of the castle looked the same as always. She sighed, relieved that there wasn't a blanket of chocolate covering the castle or the Royal Gardens.

"Doesn't look like there is any chocolate out of place here," Cocoa said.

"Look over there," Raina whispered, pointing. "It's Tula, Princess Lolli's adviser. I wonder what she's doing in the gardens so late at night."

"She's talking to a bunch of Sour Orchard Fairies," Berry said. Berry had once been scared to go to Sour Orchard. She had to find Lemona the Sour Orchard Fairy, who had created the heart-shaped candies Berry found by Chocolate River. After Berry met her, she found out that those fairies weren't so different from Berry and her friends. Berry squinted her eyes. "I think that might even be Lemona!"

Just then Tula flew into the castle, and Lemona was left standing in the gardens.

"I'm going to ask her what's going on," Berry said. Before Cocoa or the others could react, Berry was at Lemona's side. And then in a flash, Berry was back with news.

"Lemona said that the Sour Orchard was covered in chocolate syrup. Princess Lolli is very concerned about the chocolate mess. She said she'll cancel the Sugar Ball! There can't be a royal celebration when so many parts of the kingdom are under a chocolate spell."

"Oh, this means we're in hot chocolate," Cocoa mumbled. She twisted a strand of her long, dark hair around her finger.

"We need to break this spell immediately!" Berry shouted.

"But first we need to find out who has the wand," Cocoa added quietly.

CHAPTER

5

Chocolate Bash

The place Cocoa wanted to check first was Gummy Forest. Raina hadn't seen any chocolate in the forest before she got Cocoa's message, so maybe that was the next place for a chocolate attack. If Cocoa and her friends followed the chocolate, they'd find the wand. And right now Cocoa knew they had to find that wand before all of Sugar Valley was put under a thick, gooey spell!

The moonlight made Gummy Forest look different. Even though Cocoa had been there many times, in the dark the gummy trees and bushes took on spooky shapes. There were chocolate puddles along the ground, and random flowers and berries were chocolate-covered.

Whoever had the wand didn't really know how to handle it—or the magic. The syrupy chocolate was aimed all over the place, and not with a real purpose, the way a Chocolate Fairy would use the wand. Cocoa sighed as she flew through the trees hoping to find her next clue. She had never seen Gummy Forest in such a state. Looking over at Raina, she saw her Gummy Fairy friend was trying to be brave.

"Once we find the wand, I promise to help clean up this mess," Cocoa told Raina. "I am so sorry."

Raina glanced over at Cocoa as they flew. "It's not your fault," Raina said. "The wand falling out of your bag was an accident."

Cocoa lowered her head. She still felt responsible for the chocolate mess.

And then she saw something that made her heart stop.

In a hammock between two large gummy trees, Cocoa spotted Mogu. She froze and put her hand up to alert her friends. The five fairies huddled in the air just above the troll. Mogu

was just as Cocoa had remembered him: lying down stuffing his mouth full of chocolate. His hands and face were stained with dark splotches of chocolate, and his large nose was sniffing a chocolate-covered gummy flower. He was making loud slurping sounds as he ate all the chocolate around him.

Cocoa took a deep breath. She tried to summon all the courage that she could. After watching Princess Lolli in Black Licorice Swamp, she knew she had to be brave as well as clever to trick this hungry old troll. She motioned for her friends to stay where they were, and she got ready to fly down to face Mogu.

Melli grabbed her hand. "Do you want me to go with you?" she asked.

Cocoa shook her head. "No, I need to do this

alone. It's my chocolate wand, and I'm going to get it back."

Her friends all exchanged looks, but they knew that when Cocoa got stuck on an idea, that was the end of the discussion.

"I'll be fine," she said. "I've talked to Mogu before. This time, I know what I need to do. Besides, I know you are right behind me."

"Sure as sugar," Melli said, smiling.

Cocoa flew down to the hammock and took a deep breath.

"Mogu," Cocoa said as she landed next to him. She was surprised at how calm and sure she sounded.

"Ah, the little Chocolate Fairy!" Mogu said. *"Bah-haaaaa,"* he laughed. "I see you have been busy. I love what you've added to this place. I always thought this forest needed a little more chocolate."

Mogu's ring of white hair around his head was sticking up. And his dark, beady eyes were wide with greed. Cocoa tried to steady her breath. She felt as if there was a fire in her belly, heating her up.

Be calm, she thought.

"What are you doing here?" Cocoa asked.

"I'm having an old chocolate bash," Mogu laughed. "What does it look like I'm doing? These chocolate-covered gummy berries are pretty, pretty good." He licked his fingers. *"Bah-ha-ha-haaaaaaa!"*

Cocoa stared at Mogu. He seemed to be on the verge of eating too much chocolate. He didn't look scary. His stomach looked too full of chocolate to allow him to get up. And he had that crazed chocolate gaze in his eyes that she remembered from when she and Princess Lolli had gone to Black Licorice Swamp. He was close to going into a chocolate slumber. Cocoa hoped that wasn't too far off. Then she could search for the wand without his noticing.

"I never would have thought to cover these candies in chocolate!" Mogu said with a loud burp. He reached his hand down and scooped up a bunch more berries.

Cocoa shot her friends a look. Maybe Mogu was *eating* the chocolate, not *making* the chocolate. She scanned the area and didn't see the wand anywhere. Suddenly Cocoa was encouraged. A lost wand was one thing, but it was another thing if a sour troll had it. And the only thing Mogu seemed to have was a chocolate appetite!

"Maybe you'd like some more chocolate?" Cocoa asked.

She could tell her friends were confused by her offer, but Cocoa suddenly felt very confident.

"Bah-ha-haaaaaaaa!" Mogu laughed. "I would love that!"

"Well, if you had a magic wand, you could make your own chocolate," Cocoa said. She watched Mogu's face carefully. "You wouldn't need a fairy to make the candy for you."

Mogu stopped eating and stared at Cocoa. "What a big idea from such a small fairy," Mogu muttered. "I want one of those!"

"I bet you would," Cocoa said, smiling. She was so relieved that Mogu didn't have the wand that she touched a gummy flower and gave the

candy a rich, dark chocolate shell with chocolate sprinkles. "Here," she said. She handed the greedy troll the special treat. "Try this."

Mogu ate the candy as Cocoa flew up to her friends. "Mogu doesn't have the wand!" she exclaimed.

"Why'd you give him more candy?" Dash blurted out.

"Because the faster Mogu falls asleep, the sooner he'll stop eating all of Gummy Forest!" Cocoa said, winking at Dash.

"And we've got work to do. We can't spend all day troll-sitting!" Raina said.

Cocoa was thankful to have her friends around her. Together, they would find a way to stop this chocolate spell from spreading all over Sugar Valley.

CHAPTER
6

Chocolate Storm

The five fairies watched Mogu sleeping. His mouth fell open, and he began snoring loudly. His chocolate-covered hands dangled off the hammock. With each breath he took, his big belly went up and down. Cocoa was right. The greedy troll's chocolate slumber had begun.

"Now Mogu won't eat all of Gummy Forest!"

Raina declared happily. She sent a sugar fly to Candy Castle with news of Mogu's appearance in the forest. The Royal Fairy Guards would safely fly the sleeping Mogu back to Black Licorice Swamp. The troll would not be eating any more of the Candy Fairies' candy for a while.

Meanwhile the five friends flew back to Raina's home. They needed a place to think and figure out what to do next.

"Before we start following clues all over Sugar Valley, we need to figure out a plan," Berry said.

Cocoa knew her levelheaded friend was right, but she was anxious to sget out and see if there were more chocolate clues. She couldn't help but feel this chocolate mess was all her fault. The faster she found the wand, the faster this would all be over.

"Raina, maybe we should see if anything like this has ever happened in Sugar Valley before," Melli said. "I know you said that you couldn't remember anything in the Fairy Code Book, but maybe we can help you look." She glanced over at the wall of books in Raina's room.

"I'm thinking," Raina replied. She was staring at her large bookcase. "There might be something in one of these books." She flew up to the top shelf and then glided back down with three yellow books in her hands. "I remember some kind of chocolate storm. It's barely mentioned in the Fairy Code Book, but maybe the story is in here."

"Why isn't the story in the Fairy Code Book?" Dash asked, peering over her shoulder.

Raina shrugged. "Sometimes there is more to a story than the Fairy Code Book records," she

said. She opened up one of the yellow books. Dust flew from the covers. "Sweet sugar!" she said, blowing away the dust. "I guess I haven't opened this in a while!"

"Are these stories all true?" Cocoa asked.

"I believe that they are," Raina said. "And I think I just found the chocolate storm story!"

Cocoa raced forward to sit next to Raina. All the fairies huddled around as Raina began to tell the story. The way Raina read the story, it felt as if they were all there.

"The sky was filled with dark clouds, and all the fairies in Sugar Valley knew that a winter storm was coming," Raina read. "All the sugar flies were buzzing with the news of terrible weather. Fairies snuggled inside and prepared for the winter storm."

"Yum. I bet they were all drinking hot chocolate with marshmallows!" Dash blurted out. "And the slopes on the Frosted Mountains must have been *so mint*!"

Cocoa smiled at Dash. Even at a time like this, Dash was happy to think about sweets and sledding.

"The snow that fell that day was different from other winter storms," Raina continued to read. "The normal winter white snow that usually fell in Sugar Valley didn't come. Instead, the snow was a deep, brown chocolate powder and piled up in high drifts around the valley."

"So they could just make hot chocolate by sticking their cups in the snow!" Dash interrupted.

"Shhh," Melli scolded gently. "Let Raina finish."

Raina looked over at Dash and winked. Then she read more. "The storm lasted for a week. No one knew what to make of the weather. But the fluffy sweet powder was nothing that anyone had ever seen before."

Cocoa leaned over to the book and read the next line with a heavy heart. "Some said it was a gift," she read. "And others said it was a curse. Sugar Valley was under a chocolate spell."

"So mint," Dash said. "I would have had plenty to make out of chocolate snow! Peppermint and chocolate is delicious!"

"The chocolate snow stayed around for weeks," Raina read, turning the page. "Many fairies were cooped up inside their homes. Most fairies learned how to make all sorts of chocolate treats using the powdered chocolate. They had to use the snow. There was so much chocolate!"

"What happened?" Berry asked.

Melli inched forward. She bit her nails. "Go on, Raina," she said. "Tell us what happened."

"The chocolate snow started to melt," Raina said. "There were great chocolate floods, and Chocolate River overflowed."

"What a chocolate mess!" Melli muttered.

Raina nodded and continued to read. "The snow seeped into all the sugar soil."

"Oh no," Melli said. "The crops!" Her hand flew to her mouth.

"The spring and summer crops all had a hint of chocolate," Raina read. "It took two whole years to rid the soil of the chocolate taste."

"Bittersweet," Cocoa said, shaking her head. "Too much chocolate is never a good idea."

Berry stood up and walked around. "Do you think the chocolate syrup puddles we saw are going to ruin the candy crops?"

Melli shot Berry a look.

"What?" Berry said. "I'm just asking."

Cocoa lowered her head. "Berry is asking a good question," she said. She knew that Melli didn't like it when the friends didn't get along, but Cocoa couldn't be mad at Berry for stating the truth. The crops were in danger. This situation was more serious than the Sugar Ball being canceled. They had to fix this problem quickly before the chocolate spread all over Sugar Valley.

Raina closed the book.

Cocoa sighed. Now what were they going to do?

CHAPTER 7

Chocolate Thoughts

Cocoa fiddled with her chocolate dot bracelet. No one said a word after Raina finished reading the story of the great chocolate storm. Cocoa lifted her eyes from her wrist and glanced at her four friends. Their worried expressions made Cocoa uneasy. The missing chocolate wand could ruin all the candy in Sugar Valley.

At that moment she almost wished that Mogu had stolen the magic chocolate wand. At least she had some idea how to handle the salty old troll. But now she felt helpless.

Just then Cocoa felt Melli's arm around her. "We need to find the wand, that's all," she said quietly.

"Melli's right," Berry chimed in. "This isn't a huge chocolate snowstorm. Chances are, these chocolate puddles will dry up quickly. The candy crops will be fine."

"We don't know that," Cocoa whispered.

"Let's see what we do know," Raina said. She took out a notebook and started writing. "There's a missing magic chocolate wand. And chocolate from Sour Orchard all the way to Gummy Forest."

 275

"Someone has definitely gotten hold of the wand. Someone who is clearly not a Chocolate Fairy," Dash said.

Melli flew over to Dash and gave her a tight squeeze. "That's it!" she shouted. "What we need is a Chocolate Fairy to make another wand to clean up the mess! A new magic wand could get rid of the chocolate spell."

"She'd need the first wand to be able to reverse the spell," Raina said, shaking her head.

"But maybe I could make something to help clean up the mess," Cocoa blurted out. "I just can't sit here wondering what to do." She stood up. "Send a sugar fly if you hear or see anything," Cocoa told them. "I'm going back to Chocolate Woods."

"Do you want company?" Melli asked.

Cocoa fluttered her wings. "Maybe in a little while," she said. "For now I need to concentrate on chocolate thoughts."

As Cocoa headed back to Chocolate Woods, she was saddened to see all the puddles of chocolate in Sugar Valley. Berry was right . . . whoever had the wand was not a Chocolate Fairy. A Chocolate Fairy would know how to hold the wand with better aim and skill. She shook her head. But what Candy Fairy would want to steal her wand?

Before Cocoa went into Chocolate Woods, she decided to sit on Caramel Hills to think. She was happy to see that there was no sign of chocolate on the golden hill.

Cocoa sat and wondered what would happen to the crops and thought about how sad all the fairies would be if there was no Sugar Ball. A tear fell from Cocoa's eye. How could she even tell Princess Lolli? To think that she had once been so excited about her chocolate royal wand!

Out of the corner of her eye, Cocoa saw a flash of chocolate. At first she thought she was seeing things. But then she realized—there was a chocolate clue happening right in front of her!

She got up and flew toward the caramel tree dripping with chocolate. She touched the chocolate. The thin chocolate was like syrup.

How strange, she thought. *The wand must be nearby.*

She flew up to the top of the tree and looked around. This had to be a fresh hit. The chocolate hadn't been there before. Her wings began to flutter. Was this the final chocolate clue? She scooted to the edge of the tree branch and scouted the area. She didn't realize it, but she was holding her breath. She was nervous and excited at the same time. Right beside a small chocolate oak tree she spotted her chocolate royal wand!

The sight took her breath away, and she gasped out loud. Cocoa saw the wand—and knew the fairy holding it!

CHAPTER 8

The Power of Chocolate

Cocoa flew down to the small chocolate oak. Her eyes never left her chocolate wand. "Cara, what are you doing with that?" she asked the small Caramel Fairy. Melli's little sister stood wide-eyed, staring back at her.

"Oh, Cocoa!" Cara cried. Tears sprang from her eyes and she sobbed so hard that Cocoa couldn't understand a word she was saying.

At that moment Cocoa wasn't angry at all. She reached out, took the wand, and put her arm around the young fairy. "Why don't you start at the beginning and tell me what happened?" she asked gently. She guided Cara over to a rock and sat her down.

Cara still hadn't stopped crying. "Please stop," Cocoa begged her. "If we are going to fix this mess, we have to know what happened."

Cara sniffled and took quick breaths to try to calm down. "Please don't tell Melli or Princess Lolli," she said. She looked up at Cocoa. "I really am so sorry for this mess that I've made."

"Cara, just tell me what happened," Cocoa begged. She gave Cara's shoulder a tight squeeze. "I promise I won't be mad."

Cara's shoulders relaxed and she was able to breathe easier. "Well," Cara began, "I saw your wand on the ground after Sun Dip. It was sticking out of one of the licorice bushes by Red Licorice Lake." She wiped her eyes with her hand. "I was going to give it back to you. That's why I picked it up." Her brown eyes glanced at the wand now in Cocoa's hands. "But the wand is just so beautiful."

"It's the power of chocolate," Cocoa said. "It's very hard to resist."

Cara nodded. "Yes," she agreed.

"And so you tried it out?" Cocoa asked.

"I didn't realize the magic was so strong," Cara went on. "As soon as I picked up the wand, things started to change into chocolate." The Caramel Fairy sniffled. "And the more I tried to stop that from happening, the more chocolate I made!"

Standing up, Cara walked over to the chocolate oak and leaned against the tree. "I wanted to fix what I had done, but I couldn't," she explained. "I went to find one of Raina's books. I thought I could find the answer without anyone knowing what I had done."

"Why didn't you just come to me or to Melli?" Cocoa asked.

Cara looked down at her golden brown shoes. "I wanted to fix my mess by myself," she said.

"Oh, Cara." Cocoa sighed. "You should never

be scared to tell a friend that you need help."

Pulling her hair away from her face, Cara let out a long sigh. "I guess," she said. "But at the time, I thought Raina's books could offer a quick fix." She let her hair fall around her shoulders.

"Those books don't always have the answer," Cocoa said sadly.

Cara paced around the tree. "When I got to Gummy Forest, Mogu was there!" she said. "I had never seen a troll up close before. He was so salty! I panicked and caused a chocolate explosion."

Cocoa flew over to Cara and took her hand. "Yes, I've seen Gummy Forest." She guided the young fairy back to the rock. "And then why did you go to Sour Orchard?"

"I remember hearing that Berry went to see Lemona the Sour Orchard Fairy," Cara said.

"Lemona was able to help Berry with those sour heart candies that she found by Chocolate River."

Cocoa remembered how difficult that journey had been for Berry. Berry was afraid to go to a different part of Sugar Valley. Raina had gone with her, and together they had found the Sour Orchard Fairy. And Cara, who was much younger, had gone by herself! Poor Cara, she really was trying to do everything alone.

"I didn't get very far into Sour Orchard when the wand starting oozing chocolate syrup," Cara told Cocoa. "Then I knew that I was really in a mess." She hung her head. "I heard the sugar flies buzzing about the Sugar Ball being canceled, and I got scared. I couldn't believe I had caused so much trouble. I came back here and thought I'd be safe in Chocolate Woods."

The wand in Cocoa's hands sparkled in the sunlight. The candy jewels were catching the sun's rays, and the fairy etched in the round globe was smiling. When she'd had the idea for the Sugar Ball accessory, Cocoa had never dreamed that the wand would create so many problems. Cocoa looked back at Cara's sad face.

"I thought it would be fun to try to be a Chocolate Fairy," Cara said softly. She was staring down at her hands. "At least for a little while."

"Just because you are a Caramel Fairy doesn't mean that you can't work with chocolate," Cocoa told her. "Melli and I work together all the time. But trying to make chocolate? You're going to have to leave that to the Chocolate Fairies."

Cara nodded.

"You know, when I was younger, I really wanted to be a Gummy Fairy," Cocoa told her. "I was so jealous of all the colors that Raina got to play with. Her candies were all the colors of the rainbow. Chocolate only has a few shades, you know."

"Really? You wanted to be a different kind of fairy?" Cara asked. Her eyes were wide with disbelief.

"Yes, even though I am one hundred percent chocolate!" Cocoa exclaimed. "As you can imagine, my trials didn't work out so well." She laughed to herself as she recalled her attempts. "My candies were not very good or tasty. I learned an important lesson. Candy Fairies can enjoy all kinds of candy in Sugar Valley, but when it comes to making candy, we need to stick with what comes naturally."

Cara giggled. "Well, I believe that. I can't seem to aim right or make anything except chocolate puddles!"

Cocoa was happy to see a smile appear on Cara's face. She held out her hand to her. "Come on," Cocoa said. "Let's let everyone know the wand has been found and get Sugar Valley cleaned up."

For the first time since the wand had disappeared, Cocoa had hope that the Sugar Ball still had a chance of happening.

CHAPTER 9

Chocolate Cleanup

Cocoa stood by the chocolate oak tree and watched Cara and Melli. She wanted to give the sisters a few minutes together. After Cara had calmed down, Cocoa pleaded with her to let Melli know what had happened. Just as Cocoa expected, Melli was in Chocolate Woods in a flash once she got the sugar fly message.

Knowing Melli, she would feel terrible that Cara hadn't come to her for help.

Melli's arm was around her sister as the little fairy told her story. After they hugged, Cocoa flew over to them.

"I sent a sugar fly to Candy Castle," she told the sisters. "I wanted to let Princess Lolli know that there was no chocolate spell, just a chocolate mess." She looked at Cara. "I didn't get into all

the details," she said. "So if you want to tell her what happened, that can be your choice."

Cara smiled. "Thank you, Cocoa," she whispered. "And I promise I will tell her. I don't want her to think that any of this was your fault."

"Licking lollipops!" Berry shouted as she sprang down beside them. "I just heard the sweet news from the sugar flies. No chocolate spell!" She swooped up in the air and then landed on her feet. "But we need a cleanup crew. Sugar Valley is still chocolate-coated."

"And we're just the fairies for the cleanup job," Dash said as she landed next to Berry.

"We came as soon as we heard the good news," Raina added. She hovered above her friends.

Cocoa laughed. "You see, Cara," she said, "you always need your friends around to lend a helping hand."

"Sugar flies really do get the news out in Sugar Valley," Cara said.

"Sure as sugar!" the fairies said together, laughing.

Feeling a boost of energy, Cocoa took charge. "We should each take a part of Sugar Valley to cleanup. The faster we get the chocolate off the ground, the better the chance for the crops."

"And for making sure that the Sugar Ball happens tonight," Melli added.

The fairies all stood together in agreement.

"I'll take Gummy Forest," Raina said.

"Consider Fruit Chew Meadow cleaned," Berry said.

"Peppermint Grove will be chocolate free after I'm done!" Dash exclaimed.

"Cara and I can help out in Sour Orchard," Melli offered. She grabbed her sister's hand and gave it a tight squeeze.

"And I'll take care of Red Licorice Lake," Cocoa added.

"Sounds like we've got a plan," Melli said.

"Hopefully we'll have a Sugar Ball to attend too!" Dash said with a grin. "Now that there is no spell, we can have a party tonight."

"But first we need to make sure all the crops are safe," Cocoa said. "The chocolate puddles haven't been sitting too long, so maybe there won't be any damage."

Raina agreed. "I think we have a good chance," she said. "From what I have read, the chocolate

 295

hasn't been on the ground long enough to change the crops."

"Let's all meet back at Candy Castle at Sun Dip," Cocoa told her friends. "That should give us enough time to clean up and then talk to Princess Lolli."

"Oh, I hope she'll let us have the ball," Dash mumbled.

"Me too," Cocoa whispered.

The large orange sun touched the top of the Frosted Mountains. Cocoa was exhausted. Cleaning up after a chocolate mess was not an easy task. Every part of her body ached from the tip of her wings to the bottom of her toes. She looked around at the sugar sand shoreline of Red Licorice Lake. Not a drop of chocolate in sight. Cocoa sighed. She hoped her friends had had the same luck in their spots.

When Cocoa found her friends, they all looked just as worn out as she felt.

"Chocolate cleanup completed," Raina announced when she saw Cocoa. "There was no damage to the gummy crops that I saw."

"Fruit Chew Meadow was fine too," Berry said.

"I think everything is going to bc okay," Dash agreed.

Cara stood up. "Melli and I took care of Sour Orchard," she told Cocoa. "Everything looks back to normal."

Cocoa clapped her hands. *"Choc-o-rific!"* she exclaimed.

"I'm going to talk to Princess Lolli," Cara said.

Cocoa and her friends surrounded Cara.

Princess Lolli was fair and true, but telling her something like this would be scary for the young fairy.

"We'll go with you," Cocoa told her. She knew she was speaking for all her friends.

The fairies found Princess Lolli in the royal throne room. She listened to Cara's story about finding Cocoa's wand and how she couldn't stop the chocolate from spreading all over Sugar Valley.

"I am in favor of the fairies experimenting with new candies and techniques," Princess Lolli said, "but you should always ask permission. Especially if magic is involved."

Cara nodded her head. "I promise never to try that trick again," she vowed. "From now on, I'm sticking with caramel."

"A fine choice for you," Princess Lolli told her. "You are a good Caramel Fairy, Cara. You are full of sweetness, and I know you didn't mean any harm to the kingdom."

Melli took Cara's hand. "Please don't ever feel that you can't come to me for help."

"All of us are here for you," Cocoa said. "Sure as sugar."

Cara smiled as she looked at the fairies around her. "Thank you," she said. "I promise."

Princess Lolli glanced up at the large candy clock on the wall. "Sun Dip is over, and now it's getting late." She turned to look at the other fairies. "What do you think about getting on with the Sugar Ball?"

The fairies all cheered.

"Those are some extra-sweet words!" Cocoa

cried. "I can't wait to wear my new dress." She put her hands on her hips. "But maybe I should leave my chocolate wand at home."

Everyone laughed, but Princess Lolli shook her head.

"You've worked very hard on that wand, Cocoa," the fairy princess said. "Please don't leave the wand at home."

Cocoa's wings fluttered, and she couldn't help but smile. "I would love to bring my chocolate wand tonight. And I won't be letting it out of my sight the whole night!"

CHAPTER 10

Chocolate Dip

The grand ballroom at Candy Castle was glorious. The entire room was glowing with tiny sparkling white sugar lights. Each table was covered with a white tablecloth with tall sugar blossom branches in brightly colored gummy vases. The tiny white flowers on the branches were shimmering with colored sugar.

The room had never looked so sweet.

Cocoa twirled around in a circle in front of her friends.

"The dress is delicious," Berry remarked.

Blushing, Cocoa smoothed out the skirt. "Thank you," she said. "A comment like that from you is extra-sweet."

Across the room Cocoa saw Cara. She was wearing a short dark caramel dress with a sparkling tiara in her hair. Cocoa flew over to her and noticed that the sweet tiara was covered in tiny caramel drops.

"Your tiara is extraordinary," Cocoa told her.

Cara curtsied. "Thank you. I may not be able to handle chocolate, but I am learning how to make caramel candy!"

"Well done," Cocoa cheered.

Princess Lolli came over to Cocoa and Cara. Her pink-and-white-sugar layered dress looked scrumptious. In her left hand, Cocoa noticed the royal wand. Princess Lolli's wand was made entirely of sugar crystals. The wand was dazzling with the sugar-frosted jewels. Cocoa couldn't take her eyes off it.

"I see you did bring your chocolate wand," Princess Lolli said to Cocoa. "I'm glad that you did. Your work is excellent. You should be proud."

"Thank you," Cocoa said. "And I'm not letting the wand go!" She laughed. "No more crazy chocolate episodes in Sugar Valley."

"Let's hope not," Princess Lolli said, grinning.

Cara held her hand up to her chest. "Certainly not from me," she vowed.

Princess Lolli winked at her. "Enjoy the party,"

she said as she flew to greet more guests.

"Look," Melli cried as she raced over to Cara and Cocoa. "It's the Sugar Pops! They really are here!" She pointed to the far corner of the room, where a stage was set up.

"Where are the Sugar Pops?" Dash and Berry exclaimed from behind Melli. She looked all around.

Raina landed next to Dash. "The Sugar Pops are here already?" she asked.

Melli laughed. "They are right there," she said. She put her hands on their shoulders and faced them in the right direction.

Once everyone saw the brothers, they let out a sigh.

"Now the party can really begin," Coca said, smiling.

"Char is just so yummy," Melli said with a sigh. "Look at that hat. He is just the sweetest."

Dash flew up above her friends to get a better view. "I don't know," she said. "I think Chip is just delish."

Cocoa laughed. "Well, together those three have the best sound in Sugar Valley. Let's go say hi to them."

Melli pulled at Cocoa's hand. "Do you think they will remember us?" she asked.

"Hot chocolate!" Cocoa exclaimed. "Of course they will remember! How could they forget the fairies who saved Caramel Moon?"

The four friends laughed and followed Cocoa over to the front of the stage.

Just as Char, Carob, and Chip took center stage, Cocoa caught Char's eye. He grinned down at her and then whispered in his brothers' ears.

A hush fell over the crowd. Everyone wondered what the Sugar Pops were up to. Char grabbed the microphone and greeted the crowd.

"Hello, Candy Kingdom!" he sang out. "Happy Sugar Ball! We're so happy to be here today now that the chocolate mess has ended." A roar of cheers and applause echoed in the room. "And we'd like to call up five of our fairy friends to help us with our first song, 'Chocolate Dip.'"

"'Chocolate Dip' is my favorite song!" Cocoa exclaimed. She grabbed her friends, and they all flew to the stage. They were so excited to be close to the famous singers again. Cocoa reached out and took Cara's hand. "Come with us!" she shouted.

Char nodded and the music started. The

friends huddled together and swayed to the music. Looking out at the crowd, Cocoa saw that everyone was having a great time. She waved her wand at the end of the song, and tiny chocolates fell around the Sugar Pops. The boys laughed and threw the candies out in the crowd.

"Nice touch, Cocoa," Char whispered. "That is some wand!"

Cocoa thought her heart would melt!

"Oh, you have no idea," Melli mumbled. Laughing, Melli gave Cocoa a tight hug.

The Sugar Pops went on to play all their hits. All the fairies in the kingdom were rocking out to their sweet sounds. The Sugar Ball was a great success, and everyone was having a supersweet time.

Cocoa went over to Cara and put a chocolate

drop in her hand. "If you ever need any chocolate, please never hesitate to ask me," she said.

"Don't worry," Cara told her. "I know where to find my chocolate. You have my word that I will be more responsible."

"Sure as sugar," Cocoa said. "This is the best Sugar Ball ever!"

She twirled Cara out on the dance floor. "Maybe we can work on some caramel and chocolate candies together."

"I would love that," Cara said, smiling.

"Me too," Melli said, coming between them. "Count me in."

"Count us all in!" Dash exclaimed.

"The more fairy friends, the sweeter!" Cocoa announced. And then she fluttered her wings and spun around to the music.